RITUALS AND THE RESTLESS REMAINS

A WILLIAMS WITCH MYSTERY

BOOK EIGHT

ELOISE EVERHART

ALORIUM PUBLISHING

PB ISBN: 978-1-962759-07-6

Author: Eloise Everhart

Editors: Rashida Breen and Kelly Reed

Cover design by GetCovers

CHAPTER 1

My muscles strained as I hoisted a wooden booth up from the wooden floor of the Bizzy Bean Cafe. Megan grunted next to me as we took a faltering step backward. The wood dug into my fingertips as it dipped down on the side.

"Steady," I said.

The Retirees let out a slew of curses under their breath as they struggled to keep it upright.

"A little bit more to the left." Heather stepped up next to the Retirees and lifted with them.

With the four of them on one side and Megan and me on the other, the large wooden monstrosity leveled out, and we shuffled back a few more inches. My back hit the surround, and my arms shook as Megan slipped out from her position so that we could nudge it the last two inches into place. As we set the wooden booth down, I slumped back into the hidden alcove behind it and let out a shaky breath. I ducked down and crawled out from behind the booth, my fingers tracing the metal strip embedded into the floor. *Strip* was probably the wrong word. It was more like a braid. Thin strands of silver, gold, and iron wound around each other were set into the wood. I scampered out, dusted off my knees, and turned in place to admire our work.

Over the last week, we had replaced every table at the Bizzy Bean with ones custom built by Megan. Each table had flowers and crystals spread over them in an artistic pattern, with resin over the top to keep it all in place. The epoxy gleamed under the lights, with little flecks of yellow mica suspended in the mix. The tables were beautiful. And the crowning jewel of the whole space was the massive booth at the back of the room. We had pulled out two booths and replaced it with one large enough for our entire coven to sit down at the same time. It had the same resin countertop as the other tables, but we had taken a step further with it. A ring of metal surrounded it, embedded into the floor, and hidden under that at each of the corners was a small pocket that hid mercury thermometers. It was a space specifically designed for us to be able to meet and cast spells without the rest of the cafe noticing. And it was gorgeous.

"I love it," I whispered.

Megan ducked her head. In the back of my mind, through our coven bond, I could sense her happiness. But she was too humble to ever acknowledge her good work. She had spent the better part of six months working with Heather, handcrafting everything there to meet the Bizzy Bean aesthetic while still being useful for our magical purposes.

I bumped her with my hip. "We should test it."

Agnes groaned behind me. "Can't that wait until tomorrow? All this physical labor is exhausting."

"Dani's right. We might as well get it out of the way," Betty grumbled. "Otherwise, I'm going to be dreaming about moving tables around."

"I offer myself up as the first test subject." Sarah flopped into a chair at a neighboring table and waved her hand at the booth. "Go. Practice. And if I don't hear anything suspicious, we'll know it's good."

The rest of us shuffled into the booth. Betty slid in first, scooting around to the center, and stared out at the room. I took the last seat, facing Heather. I shifted in my seat to see the rest of the room. The Bizzy Bean had changed a lot since I moved across Washington state to Point Pleasant about a year before. Heather had changed it into a cat cafe. Half the space was enclosed in plexiglass. The decorations had shifted from entirely bee themed, to incorporating cats playing with or chasing bees. The right-hand wall was almost entirely taken up by a massive cat structure that was more of a cat castle than a tower. With each change, the cafe felt more and more like home.

I let my hand dip and touched the ring of metal next to me and muttered the words of the spell to prevent eavesdropping. Motes of light swirled out of my mouth and settled into the metal ring around us. Agnes took up a spell next to me. Iridescent shimmers filled the air, creating an illusion around the table of us discussing something innocuous like the weather. The lights settled around us, leaving a shimmering veil over the table.

"Okay. What should we say to test this thing out?" I asked.

"Sarah is a terrible cook who wouldn't know how to make French toast if her life depended on it." Betty stared at Sarah as the words left her mouth.

Sarah continued to sit there, a bored expression on her face.

"The Dewey decimal system is superior to the Library of Congress system." Agnes added, cocking her head to one side as she watched for any reaction from the other table.

I covered my mouth, trying not to laugh. Sarah might have been able to ignore the French toast comment, but she would never overlook an affront like that. She had spent too many years working at the local college library to let that insult slide. Last time it came up, she had ranted for almost an hour about the pros and cons of both in an attempt to illustrate how much better the Library of Congress system was at organizing books. "I think we're good."

We dropped the spells, the shimmering lights vanishing, and slid out of the booth.

"Done already?" Sarah asked.

Heather nodded. "Like a charm."

Megan stretched. "Good. There's a hot shower waiting at home with my name on it."

"Same." I grabbed my bag and headed toward the front door. "I'll see you ladies tomorrow."

I slid behind the wheel of my car and slouched. The normal breeze coming off the Puget Sound hadn't come through that day, which left the air hot and humid. Inside my car, it was even worse. After a few seconds, sweat pooled along my spine.

I pinched the bridge of my nose. Six months had passed since I rescued my daughter, Grace, from the Outsider's influence. Learning I was a witch had been difficult. Learning that I was descended from a cursed family line had been even harder. But the thing my brain still struggled with the most was the knowledge that Outsiders existed. I found it hard to wrap my head around the idea that not only were Fae out there, but a fragment of one had been possessing my daughter. Six months before, that fragment had fled when a Warden of the West tried to banish it. And for six months, everything had been quiet, unnervingly quiet. But the persistent pressure at the back of my head, my divination ability that let me know when I was in danger or near something important, wouldn't let me relax. It was a constant reminder that the fragment was still out there, that none of us were safe.

I straightened in my seat and started my car. The anxiety at the back of my mind wouldn't let me sleep unless I checked it personally. I drove on autopilot to Meredith Walker's house, the prison that kept the bulk of the Outsider still trapped. I pulled to a stop across the street and stared up at the home. A shiver ran down my spine. Putting my finger on what was wrong with the house was hard. It was a two-story Craftsman that seemed to loom over the street, the windows a little too dark. My gaze lingered on the large crack that ran through the home's foundation. It started to the left of the front door, and if I got out to walk around the home, I could see where it exited on the other side. I tore my gaze away from it before the voices could begin whispering.

Rolling my shoulders back, I unfocused my eyes and looked back at the house. I leaned forward in my seat, my hands wrapped over the top of the wheel. With my eyes unfocused, I could see the wards enchanted into the wood of the home. Red marks swam under the surface. Chains of symbols swirled around the home, most unbroken. A few had snapped, their symbols dark and almost out of power. None of them had changed since my last visit. While something had escaped six months before, the rest of the wards remained, keeping the Outsider trapped inside. I chewed on my lip. *What broke out? If it really was Meredith, wouldn't she have done something by now?*

My gaze slid from the home to the yard. Other, newer symbols looped around the home. These looked different from the ones on the house. They were made of shimmering red globes that looked almost bloodlike. That was what Kimberly Jones's magic looked like. Intermixed with the globes were the red flower petals of Megan, the golden motes of light from me, a shimmering iridescent haze from Agnes, and flickering flames from Sarah. The blood held it all together. The rest just acted as support. Betty had been too nervous about her curse of unintended consequences messing something up, so she hadn't layered in her misshapen pearls to the mix. The ward we'd put around the home to alert us to any changes was still firmly in place.

Everything was as it should be. But the pit in my stomach expanded as I stared at it.

What is she waiting for?

The Wardens of the West had left months before. With no signs of change, they had been called back to their other duties. They seemed to feel comfortable relying on the other wards being unbreakable by anyone not trained in Warden magic. I wasn't so sure since the first one had broken and Julie hadn't been trained by anyone. I was forced to rely on the fact that every witch in town had compulsions embedded in their minds to call the Wardens if something changed. With all of us watching, one of us should notice anything suspicious.

What is she waiting for?

The pressure at the back of my head pulsed harder the longer I stared at the house. My skin crawled at the sight of those broken chains. But a necromancer had cast those wards, and that type of witch was apparently rare. Delaney, one of the Wardens, had said she put feelers out to find one powerful enough to come and redo them. After months of silence, that didn't seem to be going well.

What is she waiting for?

I ground my teeth as the whispers began at the back of my mind, my gaze held captive by the fissure in the concrete. Everything melded together. No one voice was distinct enough for me to make out what was being said. The hair on the back of my neck stood up as the pressure behind my eyes pulsed. But nothing at the house changed. It all looked the same.

I flinched as my phone rang in my pocket. I tore my eyes away from the house and fished it out. Chris's name flashed across the screen as I picked up.

"There's been a murder," Chris said.

I sat bolt upright in my seat.

"I think this one falls into the 'strange' category. Did you want to come take a look?"

"What's so strange about it?" My words felt distant as the pressure in my head spiked. I held my breath, waiting for his response.

"The victim was a medium."

This is it. Something had finally happened. My stomach dropped. *Why did something have to be a dead body?* "I'll be right there."

CHAPTER 2

The sun hung low in the sky as I pulled to a stop a block away from the address Chris had given me. It was in an old section of downtown, with two-story brick buildings lining the street. The revitalization project of the new mayor, Steven Bishop, hadn't yet reached that far. On one side of the street, the brick facades had been power washed. New murals had gone up on the sides of buildings. And on the other side, one out of every three store fronts was shuttered. The medium's business was in the non-revitalized section.

That late into summer, the sun didn't set until after eight at night. Warmth clung to the humid air, drenching me in sweat as I climbed out of the car. Chris met me halfway and pulled me into a loose one-arm hug before quickly stepping back.

"The last of the deputies left a few minutes ago," he said.

"I appreciate that you're still willing to sneak me into crime scenes with all your new responsibilities," I said. "Although, I suppose that may be one of the perks of being the acting sheriff. Hopefully?"

Sheriff Robert Wright, or Bob to most people, had taken a leave of absence six months prior after it was revealed that his father had covered up more than one murder committed by a local crime boss. I understood what it felt like to have one's family history revealed in painful ways. I had to wait until after my gran died before she told me, through a letter, that I was a witch. Being the local sheriff was a family legacy for Bob. His father had been his hero. The story was almost sad. If he hadn't spent so much time disliking me, I might have felt worse about his situation. I was sure he would be back to his old curmudgeonly self soon enough.

Chris smiled weakly. "A small perk. But that doesn't mean I want to explain your name on the log to Peggy too often."

I grimaced. Peggy Lewis had been the office manager for the sheriff's department for as long as I could remember. She did not appreciate rule breaking and would let that be known with pointed glares and disappointed sighs.

"If it's nothing, at least we'll both have peace of mind," I said. "And if it's not… I'll owe you one."

"And I would owe you one right back. I'd be totally lost trying to solve a case involving magic without you." He grabbed my hand. "Let's make this quick. Hopefully, there's nothing unusual there, and we can go back to my place to cuddle and watch a movie. We are still on for tonight, right?"

I squeezed his hand. "Yes. I made sure Grace was okay with feeding Charlie his dinner before I left this morning."

He marched me down the block. Despite the heat, I didn't pull my hand out of his. I could feel the tension in his palm. Chris was by the book in most things, but he'd made a promise to let me look at unusual crime scenes in case it was somehow related to the ghost of Meredith Walker being on the loose. The warring promises were probably stressing him out. I couldn't help but love him for choosing to uphold his promise to me. However, the fact that it was making him uncomfortable made me feel a little queasy. I squeezed his hand, trying to reassure him that he was doing the right thing. We had to know if magic was involved. If so, things could spiral quickly.

We came to a stop in front of the medium's shop. A neon sign of a hand, the palm facing outward, hung in the window. Below it, a display of leather-bound books, bundles of sage, and a half-melted candle on an obviously fake human skull took up the rest of the space. In a Gothic-style cursive script were the words Madame Halloway. I raised an eyebrow and stepped inside.

As my foot crossed the threshold, I swayed in place as nausea swept through me. I swallowed and slowed my breathing. *Why am I nauseous?* I sniffed at the air and detected a faint coppery scent intermixed with incense. Nothing malicious was obvious. I exhaled and took another step inside. I shuddered as the sensation of ants crawling over my skin overcame me. *What is that?* With each step, I felt I was walking through sludge. The roiling feeling in my stomach grew until all I could taste was the bile rising at the back of my throat.

I cleared my throat and turned my head to survey the space. It wasn't a large shop. The walls were covered with wooden display cases filled with occult paraphernalia. Rows upon rows of crystals and jars filled with herbs and dried flowers were there. In the center of the room was a circular table. On the floor next to it was an outline of where a body had been. The scene was a strange mix of things. Half of it felt like it was for show. But when I took in the various labels, almost all the various materials were legit. *Was she really a medium?* I picked at my cuticles as I turned again.

The nauseated feeling hadn't gone away. Instead, it had intensified, the closer I got to the center of the room. I took a step back and walked the perimeter. The sensation ebbed and flowed along the edges. As I approached the front door, it spiked, and as I approached the back door, it spiked again. I pressed my fingers into my forehead, smoothing my brow. I shook out my arms and cracked my neck. With some of the tension gone, I relaxed my eyes. *Show me what's hidden.*

My stomach roiled again as the magical residue came into view. A green line of slime cut through the space. It coated the center of the room, its edges indistinct as it pooled outward. I'd never seen anything like it before. It was disgusting to look at. I looked down at my feet. The slime was on my shoes. *Oh my God, it's on me.* I covered my mouth and craned my neck upward, blinking until the vision of slime slipped out of view. *How do I even get that off?* I didn't want to think about it. *Would it come off in the shower? Do I need to do some sort of cleansing ritual?* I shook my head and lowered my hands. My freak-out had to wait until later.

I controlled my breathing and stepped back into the center of the room. I trailed my fingers over the edge of the table. My heart was painfully sluggish in my chest, like it was trying to beat quickly but something was gripping it. I yanked my hand back. I couldn't get a clear read on the emotional remnants left behind on the table. I felt like touching it would be wrong. I shook out my hand and moved through the room, lightly touching various objects. With each one, that same gross feeling lingered on my fingers as I yanked my hand away. I couldn't read anything in there without feeling like I was going to throw up.

As I passed the counter at the back of the room, the hairs on the back of my neck stood up. I almost missed that sensation because of the nausea. I stepped back and forth in front of the counter, and the hairs went up and down on my neck. I studied the counter. It was sparser than the rest of the room. Business cards sat in a small stand near a flyer for a local movie festival under a glass plane, an old metal register with vintage-style keys, and a logbook. I held my hand over the counter and closed my eyes as I moved it over the various objects, focusing on my body. When I felt a slight tugging sensation as my hand moved over a specific spot, I cracked my eye open. It was the logbook.

I pulled the book toward myself and flipped it open. It was a sign-in book for consultations. I turned the pages to the last one with writing and read through the names.

Linda Sinclair
Rowan Tate
Julie Davis
Odessa Cain
Isabel Carter
Leif Navarro

I drew in a breath, and my eyebrows rose. *Isabel Carter. Izzy.* I had worked on a few cases with her since discovering I was a witch. She was a journalist for the Island County Gazette, who wrote the entertainment section. She had dreams of becoming a hard-hitting journalist. *What on earth was she doing at a place like this?* I pulled out my phone and snapped a picture of the page then pushed it back to its original position.

I stepped back from the counter and took one final look through the room. My gaze snagged on a painting on the far wall. It was of a woman with a mane of black hair and piercing green eyes, standing in front of the moon. Tree limbs crowded around her, giving her a wild look. I strode toward it. The painting had eyes. One of the spells I'd practiced enough to use without one of my notebooks was one that let me experience the past of an object from its perspective. If the object had literal or metaphorical eyes, like cameras, I could see what had happened in a space. I muttered the words to the spell as my fingers came up to the woman's face. Motes of light flowed from my lips to the painting, but nausea roiled through me as I lifted my hand,

and I gagged. The motes of light flickered and went out without settling into the canvas.

Cursing under my breath, I turned away and rested my head on the glass of a nearby display case. The coldness helped ease the worst of the queasiness. I straightened and tried again. On the third word, bile came up in the back of my throat. I swallowed it and dropped the spell. Something about this room, about the green slime, was too disgusting to try to cast around. I tried not to retch as I opened my mouth to try a third time. I couldn't do it. The feeling of wrongness was too strong. I turned on my heel and fled outside.

The sun had dipped lower on the horizon while I was inside. The heat still lingered in the air, but a cooler breeze was finally coming off the Sound, promising a more comfortable night. I leaned back against the storefront and controlled my breathing. *Okay. Casting spells inside the building is out.* I pushed myself away from the wall and studied my surroundings. If the place had been closer to newer sections of downtown, investigating would have been easier. Cameras or murals nearby could have caught something. But the newer art was just far enough away that even if the art pieces had eyes, my spell would have been useless. I groaned and spun in place, searching for something, anything, that would be helpful. My gaze landed on a storefront across the street. The lights were still on. A wooden sign hung over the door: The Well-Worn Word.

Chris trailed behind me as I marched across the street. I pushed the door open and stepped inside. Then I faltered in the doorway. Bookcases towered over me, stretching from floor to ceiling. They wound through the space. A large placard was posted on the end of the first row, with arrows pointing in various directions toward Romance, Mystery, Travel, Occult, and Register. I followed the arrows toward the register.

A man sat behind the counter, his long, lanky frame

folded in on itself as he peered down at a book in his hands. He flipped the page, a small frown crossing his face as he gripped the pages. I stopped in front of him. He started upright, dropping the book.

He pushed his large blue-framed glasses up his nose. "Didn't hear you come in. What can I help you with?"

I placed my hands on the counter and smiled up at him. He was touching it lightly on the other side.

Through the wood, I could sense his embarrassment. "I'm not sure if you heard what happened across the street—"

He swallowed. A surge of sorrow flowed into me through the counter, and tears pricked my eyes.

I blinked the tears back. "I should probably start with my name. It's Dani Williams."

"I think I've heard of you," he said.

I flushed. "You have?"

"Small town." He shrugged. "If it helps, they were good things. I'm friends with Willow."

"I'm trying to figure out what happened over there. I was wondering if you saw anything or anyone strange in the area." I swallowed and softened my voice. "It would have been something recent. Something that may have made you feel… uncomfortable, perhaps?"

He grimaced and ran his hand through his hair. "The man from this morning?"

I nodded, encouraging him to go on.

"I told the cops already. It was right before opening. I was about to flip the sign on the door when I saw him walk into her store. There was something about him. He… moved wrong? He made my skin crawl, so I hid after I saw him go inside. I didn't come out for a good twenty minutes. I never saw him come back out because I was… I was hiding. But after a while, I was too worried about her, so I went over. And that's when I found *her*." His voice cracked at the last word. Tears filled his eyes. "I really should have gone home today. But after that, I couldn't bring myself to go anywhere. I was just going to be alone with that image in my head."

I reached across the counter and patted his hand. "What did he look like?"

He shook his head. "I didn't get a good look. Six feet maybe? Dark hair. He… he moved wrong. I don't know how to describe it. He was just wrong."

I patted his hand again before reaching into my pocket and fishing out a business card. "If you think of anything else, give me a call."

He stared at my card before shoving it into his cardigan pocket. I backed away from the counter and walked out of the bookstore. The sun had finally dipped down below the horizon. I hunched my shoulders and stared at the storefront of Madam Halloway's across the street. The pink neon looked almost happy. I ground my teeth together and wandered over to Chris, who was waiting by his cruiser.

"Did you find anything?" he asked.

I shrugged. "I don't know yet. It's definitely odd. There was magic involved."

"Magic you've seen before?"

I shook my head and pulled out my phone to text my coven members. My muscles in my hands seized. I fought for control as my fingers flipped through my contact list. My index finger hovered over Miranda Blackwood's name. She was the Warden of the West who had put a compulsion on me to contact her if I found any sign of the Outsider. I gritted my teeth. *I haven't confirmed it yet. Green could mean anything. Just because Meredith's magic was green doesn't mean this is related. It was sludgy. Her magic was sparkly. Correlation does not equal causation.* My hands relaxed. I didn't trust Miranda. I would contact her if I had to, but not a moment sooner.

I scrolled back up through my contact list and selected the coven chat.

DANI:
Emergency meeting in 15. Meet me back at the Bizzy Bean.

I tucked my phone into my pocket and stepped into Chris. I wrapped my arms around him and ducked my head against his chest.

He rested his chin on my head. "I take it movie night is being canceled?"

I sighed and pulled back. "Rescheduled. Leave the light on for me? I miss your snores."

He leaned forward and gently kissed me. "Lies. I never snore."

I giggled. "I hate to break it to you—"

"Lies." He wrapped his arms around me and chuckled into my mouth as he peppered me with another kiss. "And slander."

We stood there in each other's arms until my phone dinged with a response on the coven chat. I sighed and straightened.

"I'll message you when I'm on my way over. If things go fast, maybe we'll still have time for an episode of something." I squeezed his hand and turned and walked away.

Emergency coven meetings were never fast, especially when I was dropping potentially bad news on all their heads. Correlation didn't mean causation. But magic was involved in Delilah Halloway's murder, and that was never good.

CHAPTER 3

Most of the lights were out when I parked outside the Bizzy Bean. The artwork in the window was backlit, making the white cat featured in the painting almost look black. I shuffled to the front door and knocked lightly. Heather ducked her head out from the kitchen. She walked toward the door to let me in, wiping her flour-coated hands on her apron the entire way. I darted inside, and she pulled the door closed behind me.

Heather studied me, her green eyes filled with concern. "You look like something the cat dragged in. And I should know. I have fifteen fosters right now. Are you doing okay?"

I shrugged. "Let's wait for the others. You need any help in the kitchen?"

"Always." Heather wrapped an arm around my shoulder and led me into the room where all the real magic happened. Though I wasn't a bad cook, Heather worked miracles in there. She pushed me toward one of the sinks. "Wash up first. Then help me prep for tomorrow. The baking starts at five a.m. So the less measuring I have to do first thing in the morning, the better."

I followed her directions and measured out the dry ingredients for four different cookie recipes, six different types of muffins, and a lemon bread. Before too long, Megan was rapping her knuckles against the front door. We quickly cleaned our hands and made our way out to greet her. The Retirees weren't too far behind. Both Megan and Agnes had wet hair from showers. Megan had changed into pajamas, and Agnes had on a different-colored track suit. That was the first time I saw one of the Retirees not dressed like the others. Her blue tracksuit looked out of place between the green of Betty and Sarah's. We gathered at our booth in the back and took our places at the table. Agnes made quick work of activating the protection spells to prevent eavesdropping.

Heather claimed the seat next to me. "Alright, emergency coven session number twenty-seven is in session."

"Session twenty-seven?" I spluttered.

Heather cackled. "I knew I could get you to relax with something ridiculous like that."

"Twenty-seven probably isn't too far off," Megan said.

I slumped into my seat.

"So, what is it?" Betty asked.

"There's been a murder," I began. I told them about my inspection of the crime scene. Though I attempted to hold back a shudder as I described the feeling of being inside the building, I failed. "The whole thing gives me the creeps."

The group sat in a stunned silence.

Agnes opened and closed her mouth a few times before she spoke. "Delilah's dead?"

"You knew her?" I asked.

Sarah wrapped an arm around Agnes's shoulder. "Not well. But she was a sweet lady although a bit troubled."

"She was a medium. It wore on her," Betty said.

Agnes sagged. "It made her a bit agoraphobic. Whenever she stepped out her front door, ghosts would find her. I don't think she had left the building her shop was in for years."

"Do you think it's connected to Meredith?" Sarah asked.

I shrugged. "It's the same green color. But it looks different in every other way."

Betty grunted. "We should double our checks of her house. Move to four times a day instead of two. Maybe even more."

I grimaced.

Heather shifted in her seat to catch my eye. "What do you think the best use of your time will be?"

I glanced between the other members of my coven. Meredith was a burden of all of us collectively. While I had expected our temporary coven to dissolve after we freed Grace from the Outsider's control, it hadn't. We were held together by our desire to overcome our curses—well, other than Heather. She was the only non-witch member of the coven. But we were like family, so she would stand by my side no matter what. Even if it wasn't her responsibility, she would be there.

I lowered my gaze. "We need to figure out if it's tied to Meredith sooner rather than later. And the best way to do that is to solve the case."

"Alright. Then... can the rest of you pick up Dani's shifts in the rotation?" Heather asked.

My head jerked up as Megan nodded.

"Of course we can," Betty said.

"We should play to our strengths. We can do monitoring. And you..." Sarah said as she squeezed my shoulder. "You can solve the murder."

The corners of my mouth quirked upward. They had faith in me. A part of me recognized that it wasn't entirely undeserved. I had solved several cases since I discovered I was a witch about a year before. Me chasing after killers wasn't new.

"I'll call Kim. See if she's willing to be added to the rotation, too, or… if she's willing to set up any extra protection around the prison," Megan said.

Kimberly Jones was descended from the same cursed coven as the Retirees, Megan, and me. Our curses all manifested differently. Betty's made all her magic go wrong in some way. Agnes could never leave Point Pleasant. Sarah could only access her magic on a full moon. Megan's was nasty. People instantly distrusted her. That made having friends difficult. If not for a special coffee we could make that temporarily reduced the effect of her curse, she would be entirely alone. Mine wasn't much better. I had very little control over my divination abilities. Visions assaulted my dreams. Touching things with strong emotions tied to them could be painful. I couldn't turn it off. But Kimberly's was the worst of them all. Her curse made her bones so fragile that she could break her leg just walking across the room. If she didn't maintain spells to hold herself together every second of every day, she would be in agony. Something had happened between her and the other coven members twenty years before, long before I even knew I was a witch, and she hadn't wanted to be friends since. Recent events had thawed her somewhat, but she was still cool toward me.

I cleared my throat. "Are you sure she'll be willing to do that?"

"It doesn't hurt to ask." Megan shifted in her seat. "I can appeal to her love of family. If she thinks something will help keep her daughter safe, she'll do it."

"Maybe you should ask Grace for help," Sarah said in a low voice.

I stiffened. My daughter Grace was better at looking into the past than I was. While I dreamed of potential futures, she dreamed of things long forgotten.

Agnes shifted in her seat to face me. "You said you couldn't cast at the shop. Maybe together—"

"No," I cut in. "She's still recovering. She was possessed by a fragment of the Outsider for weeks. I couldn't... I wouldn't... She's not ready."

"Are you sure about—" Betty began.

"No." I shook my head. "She's my daughter."

Betty shook her head right back at me, glaring daggers. "She's not a child anymore. She'll be mad if you keep her out of this."

"She's not ready." I ducked my head. "But... if I can't figure things out, I'll talk to her about it."

"Promise?" Sarah asked.

I nodded.

"Okay. Now that is settled, what are you going to do first?" Heather asked.

"The usual. I'll figure out who Delilah's friends and family are and talk to them. I'll start by interviewing the people on her customer list since they were there most recently." I pulled out my phone, opened the photo of the list, and handed it to Heather. "Recognize any names?"

Heather whistled. "Izzy?"

I nodded and took my phone back.

Megan glanced between us. "Who's Izzy?"

"A reporter. She's helped me out on a few cases in the past," I said.

"If she's been so helpful, why not call her first?" Megan asked.

I slumped into my seat. The last time I'd seen Izzy was after a particularly harrowing event. We'd tracked a killer into the woods, and he attacked her. She hadn't made contact with me since. I wasn't sure if she wanted to see me.

"It's complicated," I said.

Agnes drummed her fingers on the table. "Will she not want to help?"

I hesitated. In my few interactions with her, she'd been passionate about investigating. She didn't want to stay writing the entertainment section for long. She wanted to be on the crime beat. She wanted to write front-page stories. She was fiery—until that man attacked her. *Is she still fiery now?* I had a hard time picturing her being anything but. Before I could talk myself out of it, I called her.

"We're sorry, but you have reached a number that is no longer in service or has been disconnected. Please check the number and try again."

I gaped at my phone. *Disconnected? What...* My hands trembled as I searched for the newspaper's contact information. Their normal business hours were over, but I was sure someone would still be there, still working. I dialed. I went through a phone tree before I finally reached someone.

"I'm looking for an Izzy Carter," I said.

"I can't help you with that," the woman huffed on the other end. "Let me transfer you over to HR. They're not in at this hour, but leave a message, and someone might call you back."

I left a voice mail then frantically pulled the newspaper's website back up on my phone. Her picture wasn't in the journalist section. I searched for her name, and her last article had been published just over six months before. She didn't work there anymore. My fingers flew over the screen of my phone as I searched for her on social media. Almost everything was private, and her professional page didn't list anything after the Island County Gazette. Something had happened to Izzy, and I'd missed it.

"What is it?" Heather asked

I blinked down at my phone. "I don't know. I can't... She's not a reporter anymore. Why would she give that up?"

Heather pulled me into a hug. "It's okay. I'm sure there's an explanation. Maybe she's writing for someone else or... working on a book or something. I'm sure she's okay."

I nodded. A lump had formed in the back of my throat. A strange certainty settled over my shoulders. Izzy was somehow both okay and not okay at the same time. In my mind, she was fractured. Exhaustion hit, and I slumped into Heather's arms.

"It's going to be okay." Heather rubbed my back.

I nodded into her shoulder, my eyes staring blankly forward. *I've missed something important, and I don't know what it is.* I wetted my lips. "I think I need to sleep on this. I'll do my usual research in the morning."

Heather stood, and I slipped out of the booth. The rest of the coven slid around us. We stood in awkward silence.

Megan squeezed my shoulder then headed for the door. "I'll call Kim."

The Retirees followed her out. "We'll take the first drive-by of Meredith's place," Betty said from the doorway.

I nodded again as I shuffled toward the door. *What did I miss?* Heather hugged me one more time before closing it behind me. In a daze, I walked back to my car. Minutes passed as I sat there unable to shake myself out of it. Closing my eyes, I exhaled slowly through my nose. *I don't have time for self-doubt. I have a murderer to catch.* My breathing steadied. *I have a mystery to solve.* I was certain part of that would involve figuring out what had happened to Izzy. I would start as I always did, by interviewing friends and family. I would just need to think creatively to track them all down.

CHAPTER 4

The shrill ringing of the phone pierced my dreams. I sat bolt upright in bed and reached for my phone, but it was silent. The ringing was coming from the other side of the bed. Chris grumbled and swung an arm out to the side, blindly reaching for it.

On the fourth ring, he answered. "This is Harris."

I blinked back sleep from my eyes and peered at the alarm clock on the nightstand while Chris grunted his understanding to the person on the phone. The time was half past six. Early morning lit up the corners of the blinds. I threw my arm over my eyes. I'd hoped to sleep in until seven. Something was especially annoying about being woken up within half an hour of my alarm clock going off. I never had enough time to go back to sleep—not fully, anyway.

Chris's acknowledging grunts took on a concerned edge. I peeked at him from behind my arm as he sat up and grabbed a notebook from the nightstand. He jotted something down and dropped it again. "Be there in twenty." He hung up and stood.

"Everything okay?" I asked.

He yawned and stretched. "You should get dressed."

I pushed myself up on my elbows. "Is everything okay?"

"There's been another murder."

"Another weird one?"

"Not exactly." He grabbed a change of clothes and strode into the bathroom. "But the victim is."

My heart skipped a beat as I scrambled out of bed. "Who is it?"

"Dr. Adrian Reynolds." Chris started the shower.

I faltered at the name. He wasn't in my mental Rolodex, but something about it was familiar. *Reynolds? Harold Mitchell's attorney?* "Is that one of Thomas's sons?"

"It is," Chris answered through the cracked bathroom door.

I grabbed my overnight bag from the armchair in the corner and quickly changed from my pajamas into a fresh pair of jeans and a lightweight cotton blouse. Thomas Reynolds had been the attorney for Harold Mitchell, and Harold was what passed for an organized crime boss in our sleepy town. While Thomas had been dead for over a year, from a heart attack by all accounts, Harold was sitting in prison for a slew of murders. The final count had been nineteen. And the first victim had been Beau Lancaster, Meredith Walker's boyfriend. By all accounts, his death was what had turned her to the dark side. Thomas had helped cover it up, so killing his descendants would definitely be something Meredith's ghost would be interested in.

The shower turned off. Sleeping over was still somewhat new. When Grace was possessed by the Outsider, I stayed over every night for eight days straight. Since then, I'd only done so once a week. With Grace still recovering from her ordeal, I felt guilty being out of the house too much in case she needed me. For the past few months, I'd left before him. I didn't know if the request to get dressed was because he was leaving or because he wanted me to come with him. I fidgeted with my bag, waiting for him to come up. I forced myself to sit and wait. When the sink started up, I couldn't take it anymore.

"Can I come with you?" The question tumbled out of my mouth a bit too loudly.

Chris emerged from the bathroom, freshly showered and changed, with a toothbrush dangling from his mouth. I was sitting at the end of the bed, my hands folded over my lap.

He nodded. "Why do you think I asked you to get dressed?"

I slipped off the bed and padded across the room toward him. I pulled him into a hug, resting my head against his chest. "You are too good to me."

He squeezed me back before ducking back into the bathroom to rinse out his mouth. "You ready?"

"Almost." I followed him into the bathroom and grabbed my toothbrush.

I made quick work of brushing my teeth and combing out my hair. I tied it up in a low ponytail and scampered after Chris as he strode down the stairs, his much longer legs propelling him forward faster than I could comfortably follow. At the front door, he glanced back at me and slowed. He held out his hand, and we walked to our cars together. "I'll text you the address." He kissed me on top of my head and slipped into his car.

I drove behind him through town. Dr. Adrian Reynolds lived in one of the newer suburbs. It was a small gated community filled with apartment-style condos. I pulled into a parking spot next to Chris and hovered in the parking lot as he walked up and approached Harrison at the front steps of the building.

Harrison was tall and lanky. Even with his shoulders hunched, he was well over six feet tall. His blond hair was pushing regulations. It curled around his ears and fell across his forehead, almost covering his eyes.

He glanced over at me and smiled. "Morning, Dani."

I smiled back and took a hesitant step forward. Neither he nor Chris motioned me away, so I strolled forward until I was standing between them.

"The downstairs neighbor called it in. They reported hearing sounds of a struggle just past five a.m. I arrived on scene, but the doc was already dead. No sign of the perp. Victor's up there now, confirming the time of death. But it looks like it probably happened pretty soon after the call came in." Despite Harrison's boyish face, he spoke with confidence. He had been a complete rookie when I first met him, but he had really grown into his own.

Chris nodded and clapped him on a shoulder. "Good work."

Harrison ducked his head to hide his blush. Unfortunately for him, due to his height, it was hard for him to hide his face that way. It would have worked better if he had looked straight up. Maybe he wasn't as confident as he seemed.

I followed Chris up the stairs to the second floor, to a landing with a single open door. Victor, the local medical examiner, stood inside with his back to the door. His usual regency-era coat had been replaced with a lab coat the same white as his pompadour hair. He glanced over his shoulder as I peered through the doorway at the devastation at his feet. Broken glass intermixed with wooden splinters covered the dark wooden floor. The big-screen TV hung at an odd angle on the wall, the screen cracked. My mouth went dry as my gaze landed on a pool of blood. I tore my eyes away, my heart hammering in my chest. Over the years as a claims adjuster, I had inspected a lot of homes where bad things like that had happened. Seeing the spot where someone had lost their life never got any easier.

When I looked back toward the spot, Victor had moved. He was standing between me and the worst of it, his eyes sympathetic. "You doing okay?" he asked.

I nodded.

Chris stepped past me into the room. "Do you know what happened yet?"

Victor put his hand on the gurney at his side. I had somehow missed the body bag next to him. "It looks like blunt force trauma to the head, but I'll know for sure when I get him back to my office."

I swallowed and stepped to the side to let him out. Harrison jogged up the stairs to help him with the gurney. I stared at their backs as they descended the stairs. Standing that close to the door, I could already feel the wrongness in the air. I flexed my hands at my sides and breathed deeply in through my nose and out through my mouth. *Just step inside. Look around. Five minutes, that's all.* I wetted my lips and turned back toward the apartment.

"Are you sure you're okay?" Chris asked.

"If it gets too bad, I'll step back outside. If that works?"

"I can give you a few minutes to look around. I'm sure you already know, but please don't disturb anything too much. Forensics still needs to come through." Chris squeezed my shoulder and took up a position inside the front door.

"Thank you," I said. "I really appreciate you sticking your neck out like this for me."

Chris glanced behind him down the stairs. "While I wish I could say I was doing it just for you, I'm not. What's a small department like mine supposed to do about magical murders? I took an oath to protect and serve. I wouldn't be protecting the community well if I didn't use all the resources available to me at a time like this."

"I'm a resource, huh?" I was trying to tease him, but the sensation of a thousand insects crawling across my skin made it hard to concentrate.

"You will always be more than that to me. You know that, right?"

"I do." I gave him a reassuring smile and turned back toward the room.

The gross feeling I'd encountered at Madam Halloway's shop was even more intense inside the apartment. Nausea rolled through my body, and I gagged.

I slowed my breathing, willing my heart rate to calm as I rubbed my sweaty palms against my pant legs. "Get it together, Dani. You can do this," I muttered to myself.

I forced myself to take another step into the apartment. I relaxed my eyes and examined the space for magic. It was everywhere. The green slime covered almost every surface in the room. It pooled in spaces, clinging to the furniture. In the spots where a struggle had clearly occurred, it pooled so thickly that it was a three-inch glob of green goo. Bile formed at the back of my throat. I swallowed it and counted my breaths as I turned again.

It was too hard to look at. I blinked, forcing the room to revert to its normal visible form. The green goo faded from view, replaced with a large condo that had space for a lot more furniture but had been decorated by a true bachelor. A small love seat sat in front of a large TV with a gaming system under it. The space was more refined than what a bachelor in their twenties would have done. All the pieces, while sparse, were classy. The love seat was fine and plush. The two-person table off the kitchen had sleek edges, and the wood had a fine polish that shimmered under the light.

Once I had my breathing under control, I walked the space. I furtively reached out to touch various objects in the room. Much like at Madam Halloway's, the emotional residue was odd and strangely layered. I held my hand steady as I touched a spot where the goop had been especially deep. My stomach revolted at the sensations. I gritted my teeth and pushed through the urge to vomit. Two sets of emotions seemed to be warring against each other. It was a strange combination of a blind, desperate rage… and boredom. It didn't sit right in my head. *How could a person be bored and angry at the same time?* I yanked my hand away as it started to shake.

I paced the room, my gaze darting from object to object. While Adrian had good taste in art, it was all useless for my purposes. No physical or metaphorical eyes were in the room. I stopped in the middle of it, my shoulders hunched as I drummed my fingers on my leg. I could try my obsidian mirror trick to try to trigger a vision. Normally when I did that at a crime scene, I physically experienced something related to the death. With how nauseous the room was making me feel, I wasn't sure I was ready for something that intense.

My eyes flicked over the room again, and my gaze landed on the edge of a frame in the kitchen. I strode toward it and grabbed the photo from the counter. Two men stared out at me from the photo. The one on the left was taller. He was a handsome man with salt-and-pepper hair and a chiseled jawline. Next to him was a man I recognized: Kevin Reynolds. His hair was mussed, his suit a little rumpled. They looked very different from each other, one put together and stylish and the other like he had accidentally fallen asleep in his office. They both shared the same warm smile although the taller of the two had a mischievous edge to his.

I glanced up from the photo at Chris. He hadn't moved from his position at the doorway. Harrison stood behind him on the landing, watching me. I had met Kevin Reynolds only a few times, but he had been kind on both occasions. When we first met, he had been dealing with his father's estate. *And now this.*

My hands tightened around the photograph. "It's a photo of his brother."

"Has someone notified the family yet?" Chris asked.

Harrison shook his head. "I was going to do that next."

Chris glanced between me and Harrison. He held my gaze for a few seconds, one eyebrow cocked in a silent question.

I nodded, my finger sliding across the glass. My stomach hitched as I hit another spot of rage and boredom.

"I'll take care of it," Chris said.

"You sure, boss?"

I didn't hear how Chris responded as I stared down at the photo. I let my eyes relax again. The glass had a small smudge of slime on it. I set the frame down and looked around the kitchen. Other than the small smudge on the glass and a little pool at my feet, the room had no magical residue. The killer had stood where I was and had touched the glass. *But why?* As I stared at it, Chris was murmuring directions to Harrison, telling him to finish securing the scene, and to wait until forensics arrived. They exchanged notes on potential witnesses to interview. I couldn't focus on their conversation as Chris continued giving directions and making phone calls. I kept staring at the photo. *Why did the killer stand here? Is Kevin next?*

"You coming?" Chris asked.

I blinked and shuffled toward the door. "Of course."

I looked back at the photo on the counter. I couldn't cast the spell to look into the past with Harrison there. When I did, I had a tendency to stand there silently for several minutes, like I had spaced out even worse than I just had. I didn't want to give the sheriff's office more things to gossip about. My being here was enough. I didn't want to add me acting weird on top of it. I hoped I would be able to convince Chris to let me come back in the future. But until then, we had a victim's brother to talk to.

CHAPTER 5

Kevin worked a few miles northwest in Langley, along the coast of Whidbey Island. The town was much smaller than Point Pleasant, but it had a cute downtown that faced the water. Kevin's office was tucked away in an alleyway a few blocks inland. A small wooden sign was fixed to the side of the building, with an arrow pointing to the side entrance that said Reynold's Family Law in a calming blue script. I wound my fingers between Chris's, our palms pressing together as we walked hand in hand to the door.

"Thank you for doing this," I said.

He pulled my hands up to his lips and brushed a small kiss against my knuckles. "Always. I'm a man of my word, after all."

I ducked my head, my face flushing, as he dropped my hand and pushed the door open. We were greeted by the sound of sniffling. My head jerked up as I stepped into the room. It was a small waiting area with a few comfortable-looking chairs along one wall. In the middle of the space was a wooden desk, where a woman with graying hair and thick spectacles dabbed at her red-rimmed eyes with a kerchief.

"Can I... Can I help you?" the woman stuttered.

Chris took the lead and stepped up to the desk. He spoke in a low, comforting tone, his deputy's hat clasped in front of him. "We are here to see Mr. Kevin Reynolds."

Her head bobbed, and she lifted the receiver. "Kevin? The sheriff is here to see you. Are you... Are you up to seeing them?"

Chris glanced back at me, his mouth pinched into a straight line. Either something else tragic had happened, or Kevin somehow already knew. But his brother had been dead for an hour or two at most. *How?*

The woman nodded and put the receiver down. "You can go on back."

"Thank you, ma'am." Chris stepped around the table and strode toward the closed door behind her desk that led to Kevin's office.

My heart stilled in my throat when my gaze landed on Kevin sitting behind his desk. His face was tear streaked, and his light-brown hair stuck out at odd angles as though he'd just been running his hands through it. His suit jacket hung on the back of his chair, his tie was loosened, and the sleeves of his white button-up shirt were pushed up his forearms. Something about the desolation in his gaze and his rumpled appearance made his lithe frame look almost fragile.

"Deputy Harris... Dani... I... Please, sit. Are there any leads?"

"I'm so sorry for your loss." I blinked back moisture. The despair in the air was palpable. Even if I wasn't a sympathetic crier, keeping the tears at bay would've been a struggle. The sorrow wrapped around me, my throat constricting as a lump formed at the back.

Chris took a seat, placing his cap on a knee. "My condolences as well. I hope this is not a sensitive question, but can I ask how you knew? I was here to inform you of your brother's passing."

Kevin closed his eyes and pinched at the bridge of his

nose. "The um... woman? She left a few minutes ago. She asked a lot of questions."

Chris frowned. "Did she say who she was with?"

"I... no." Kevin's eyes widened. "She told me, and then said she was looking into it and had questions."

I studied Kevin out of the corner of my eye as I took in the rest of the room. It was a cozy office. Kevin's desk was L shaped and pushed against the far-right corner. Next to his desk, two seats faced each other. Along one wall were framed photographs, and along the other, closer to the desk, was a row of filing cabinets. Near the door where we had come in were paintings of peaceful landscapes. On the edge of his desk were more photos. I took a seat next to Chris and peered at one of the photos as they talked.

"Did she give you a name?" Chris asked.

Kevin grimaced. "She did, but I was in such shock I don't remember what it was."

I shifted in my seat until I could see the photo better. It was of a young man, maybe twenty, with a happy-looking pit bull at his feet. Something about the dog's boxy head made its smile look extra wide. I inched toward it, my gaze flicking between the men, the photo, and the door. It sat at an angle, so the dog's face was pointed toward the door. If Kevin didn't remember what she looked like, I might be able to at least get a look at her by casting a spell to look into the past on the photograph. Kevin was focused enough on Chris that he probably wouldn't notice me spacing out awkwardly for a few minutes.

"That's alright," Chris said. "I understand talking about this twice in a row is difficult. If you need to schedule a time to come into the station to answer some questions later, that's okay."

Kevin straightened in his chair. "The sooner you have a lead, the better. I don't know how much help I'll be, but ask away."

Chris pulled out his notepad and settled in for questioning.

I half listened as I slid my hand up to the desk to rest my hand against the glass. Motes of light floated out of my mouth and swirled lazily toward the photo. The light gathered around my fingertips as I slid them surreptitiously across the smiling face of the dog. I closed my eyes as my vision shifted to the view of the room behind me.

Kevin was walking into the room. His hair was neat and his suit freshly pressed. He held a cup of coffee in his hand. He walked toward me and disappeared to my right. A minute later, the door opened.

Kevin's voice came from somewhere behind me, which was disorienting as I was hearing him through the memory as well as his muffled conversation next to me. I focused on the words he said in the memory.

"Rita, I thought I said—"

"I'm sorry to interrupt," a woman said from the doorway.

My brow furrowed. I recognized the voice but couldn't see her yet.

"Rita stepped out for a minute. We've never met, but I've heard a lot about you. And from all accounts, you're a really great guy. I'm… I'm so sorry, Kevin."

The woman stepped into the room, and my breath hitched. Most of her hair was a muted teal color. The dye job had grown out, revealing almost two inches of strawberry-blonde hair. She hugged an oversized sweater to her small body, with faded blue jeans underneath. Dark circles under her eyes showed a lack of sleep. *Izzy.* I hadn't seen her in months. We'd worked on a few investigations together. I helped figure out what happened to a maid she found dead in her room at Bee's Bed and Breakfast. *What is she doing here? How did she find out about this?*

My focus on my spell wavered and fell away before I could hear the rest of their conversation. Izzy had been desperate to make the leap from entertainment writer to the crime beat at the local paper. *Maybe she has a police radio.* I pulled my hand to my lap and cradled it against my stomach. *Why did she look so rough?* Izzy had always been so well put together. I had never seen her without her roots touched up. I licked my lips, trying to wet my dry mouth.

"Was your brother close to anyone?" Chris asked.

My gaze flicked toward their conversation. I rested the tips of my fingers against Kevin's desk while he spoke. My chest tightened, and a sharp pain jabbed my stomach as Kevin's grief flowed through the wood into my hand. I forced my fingers to stay there to track his emotional responses.

"He had a lot of friends, a string of ex-girlfriends a mile long. People liked him. But… I wouldn't say he was close to many of them. His work made it difficult for him to form long-term attachments."

"What did he do?" I asked.

Kevin smiled weakly, a sense of pride mixed with the sorrow. "He was a plastic surgeon."

"Would any of his clients have been upset about the work he did on them?" Chris asked.

Kevin shook his head. "Highly doubtful. He specialized in burn victims and scar revision. He gave people back their faces after tragedies. They loved him."

"How about his exes?" I asked.

Kevin cocked his head to the side and shrugged. "I don't know how to describe it. He was a golden child. No one could stay mad at him for long. None of his exes could ever hold it against him when the relationships ended. I mean, he was invited to at least six of their weddings. They all knew he was a bachelor, and… the only one even close to changing that is his current girlfriend, Camille. They've been together for two years now."

"Do you have her contact information?"

Kevin reached for his phone and faltered. "Am I going to have to tell her, or will you? It... it might be best if it came from me."

"We can wait to contact her until tomorrow," Chris said.

Kevin nodded and jotted down her contact information. "She's a good kid. Well, *kid* is the wrong term. She's thirty. A grad student. I think she was the first one who could keep up with his love of art, learning, and adventure."

I picked at my cuticles as I watched him write. Adrian's murder was possibly unrelated to Meredith. *But if it was...* If it was related, she could be coming for Kevin next. Meredith was a vengeful ghost who hated people, especially anyone related to the men she viewed as having betrayed her. Kevin's dad had betrayed her.

"You should get out of town and stay with some friends for a few days," I blurted out.

Kevin's hand faltered as he held the slip of paper out to Chris. "What?"

"Losing a family member like this is difficult. You shouldn't be alone right now."

"I'll think about it. Now, unless there is anything else, I should probably call Camille."

My muscles stiffened as a surge of panic flowed through me. I tried to trace it back to where it came from. *Was it Kevin?* My brow furrowed as I realized it had come from me. *But why am I scared?* I sat, half pushed out my chair, and focused. My divination powers did weird things at times. That felt like one of them. I was about to lose a thread. *Izzy?* As I thought her name, I calmed.

"Did the woman who was here before us leave contact information?"

"Yeah, she gave me her number." Kevin pushed some papers on his table aside. "She said I should call her if I thought of anything else."

"I would love to talk to her, compare notes. Would you

mind giving her a call to set up a meeting?" I forced a polite but sad smile onto my face.

"Sure, I can tell her you would like to speak with her."

I grimaced. I had a feeling Izzy had dropped out of contact for a reason. *Would she come if she knew it was to meet me? Did we really leave things so strained?* I had thought we were friends. That panicky feeling was back. "She's a reporter. I… I'm not sure she would want to come if she knew it was talking to me. Would you mind telling her it's to speak with you?"

He studied me, his eyes holding my gaze. I held his eyes to show how sincere I was. He'd spent his life reading people as an attorney. I needed him to see me as someone trustworthy. After almost twenty seconds, he nodded and picked up his phone.

"Yeah, hi. You were just at my office. I remembered I have contact information for a bunch of his ex-girlfriends. Could we meet at the coffee shop near my office?" He grunted into the phone and made a few sounds of approval. "Sounds good. I'll meet you there in fifteen minutes."

I stood and held out my hand. "Thank you, Kevin."

His handshake was firm. "I hope you can solve this one."

Chris and I left his office and went outside in the alleyway. I pulled Chris into a hug, resting my head against his chest.

"I take it you know who you're meeting," he said.

"Izzy," I whispered.

His arms squeezed me harder. "Did you want me there, or would it be better without?"

"I think this is an interview I need to tackle alone."

He kissed me on top of my head. "Call me if things get squirrelly. I'll see you tonight?"

I nodded and stepped back and squeezed his hand. With my shoulders hunched, I shuffled away. I had always considered Izzy a friend. *But if she's a friend, why do I feel so nervous?*

CHAPTER 6

My nerves almost got the better of me as I approached the coffee shop. I faltered and paced in front of a store down the block as I debated with myself on whether showing up like that was the right thing to do. I needed to talk to Izzy, and that was the only way to do it. *Do I, though? Do I need to talk to her or just want to? Is this about the investigation or me being upset that she's investigating without me? I don't have the market cornered on being nosy.* The image of her in Kevin's office flitted through my mind. She had looked so haggard. *Or am I scared that I've been a bad friend?* I flip-flopped for over a minute before I came to the conclusion that it didn't matter. The conversation had the potential to be helpful in my investigation. And if the growing pressure at the back of my head was any indication, my divination abilities might not let me skip it.

Rounding my shoulders, I strode into the cafe. My gaze settled on Izzy at a table in the back, like a magnet drawn to metal. I wiped my palms against my pant legs and made my way over to her table. Up close, she looked even worse than she had in the memory. She had always been pale, but her skin was sallow and her lips cracked. The freckles that dusted her nose stood out. Her dark-brown eyes were flat as she looked up at me.

I slipped into the booth across from her. "We need to talk."

"Let me guess—you're on the case?" Izzy's gaze flicked between me and something over my shoulder.

I glanced back. Customers were milling about around the counter, happy to be out of the heat.

"I am."

"I assumed that's why you're here. I guess I shouldn't be surprised when bodies start falling and you show up." A ghost of a smile flashed across her face before slipping away to be replaced with a blank expression. "You are curious by nature, after all."

I placed my hands on the table, trying to get a read on her. The exhaustion on her face was real. It was bone deep, a weariness that took weeks if not months of poor sleep to develop. When we last worked together, she'd been suffering from insomnia. *Is she still struggling?* I focused on the swirl of emotions under the fatigue. I felt a heaviness in my chest and a strange quivering in my gut. Through the wood of the table, I sensed tiredness, longing, and something I'd never sensed from her before: unease.

"Are you investigating too?" I asked. My limbs grew even heavier. I fought my eyelids' urge to start drooping as the topic of an investigation seemed to drain at her energy. I kept my focus on her face as she nodded. I cleared my throat, my mouth feeling cottony. "Maybe we should work together."

The fatigue vanished as Izzy lifted her hands from the table. For a second, it was replaced by my own panic at losing the thread of the conversation. I pulled my hands away before a feedback loop started. She pinched the bridge of her nose and exhaled.

"For old times' sake," I said.

"Could you please stop talking for a second and give me a minute to think?" Izzy slumped forward and held her head in her hands.

Once she was in contact with the table again, I tentatively placed my hand back onto the wood. Something inside me hollowed out as my ribs became tight in my chest. My world spun around me as I dug into the feeling. It was another emotion I'd never felt from her before. She had always been so confident, so self-assured, that despite her being my junior for a decade, I had internally joked that I wanted to have her confidence when I grew up. But that day, something was making her feel powerless. I yanked my hands back before the emotions overwhelmed me. I sat, staring at the top of her head, waiting.

After what felt like an agonizingly long time but was probably only fifteen seconds, she looked up at me and nodded. "I can do that."

"Okay. I haven't gotten far into the investigation myself yet. Did you have any leads you were working on?" I asked.

Izzy slid forward on her elbows until she was leaning into the table. She propped her head on her hand and sighed. "Not a one."

"What do you know about the first victim, Delilah Halloway?"

Izzy closed her eyes. A single tear slid down her cheek before she wiped it away. "She was nice to me when I was having a rough time. So… where would you like to begin?"

"I usually start by interviewing friends and family. I haven't finished making my list for Delilah yet, but I've got a small one started for Adrian. I already interviewed his brother, Kevin—"

Izzy snorted.

I clamped my mouth shut. She knew that. He had called the meeting. I opened and closed my mouth a few times before I could figure out what to say. "When I saw your name on the guest book, I tried to call you, but your number was disconnected."

Izzy turned her head away from me and stared at the wall. "The next logical person to talk to for Adrian would be Camille."

I reached a hand toward her. "I even called the paper. I got the impression you don't work there anymore."

She curled inward, her hands clenching into fists as she hugged her arms to her body. "Drop it, Dani."

"Are you... okay?"

"Drop it," Izzy hissed.

"You look—"

"I needed a break, okay? It's not against the law to take a break." She leaned back in her seat, pushing her body as far away from me as she could.

What did I do? I wracked my brain, trying to think of how I could have upset her, and came up blank. Her shoulders were stiff, and she looked like she would bolt if I asked one more personal question.

"Camille is probably the best person to talk to next," I said.

Izzy relaxed her shoulders and picked up her phone. "She's an artist turned psychologist, working on her Ph.D. in art therapy. I think she has a show coming up or something."

I grabbed my phone and searched for Camille's social media accounts. They were mostly private, but she did have a robust website with a professional blog. I flicked through it, skimming article by article. Halfway down the page was a mention of her preparing at her studio on campus, but it was so buried that I wasn't sure how Izzy had found it so quickly. "We should drop by her studio for a chat, then."

Izzy nodded and grabbed her bag. "She won't be there today. We'll have to try tomorrow. Meet you there at two?"

"How—"

"She does volunteer work on Tuesdays. Going now would

be worthless." She strode toward the door. "See you tomorrow."

I stared at her back through the glass door as it slammed shut behind her. She hunched her shoulders and scurried away down the street, her hands thrust deep into her pockets. She must have already been looking into Camille when Kevin called her. I sighed and sat there for a few more minutes as I pored through her, Adrian's, and Delilah's online presence. I jotted down other potential names of friends and family before heading out for work. None of them felt like solid leads, but we had to start somewhere.

My whole body ached by the end of the day. After my ambush of Izzy, I had returned to work. My job as a property claims adjuster kept me busy. The afternoon had been spent crawling under houses, scaling a roof, and checking in on the reconstruction project at the old sheriff's station. The tour had taken me up and down the steps multiple times because the elevator wasn't back up and running. It was on track for being completed before the winter. It would be nice for Chris to work in the historic building downtown instead of in the doublewide mobile offices they'd been working out of for the last few years due to a massive water leak that had left their downtown location closed indefinitely until the new mayor, Steven Bishop, decided to revitalize the neighborhood.

I grabbed the Slice of Life Diner to-go bag from the front seat and heaved myself out of my car as Grace pulled across the street. I waited for her, letting my body relax against the warm metal of the car door.

"I hope you guys don't mind Dominion. I couldn't find Settlers of Catan." Grace held up a stack of board game boxes.

"Sounds great to me. You need a hand?"

Grace shook her head. "I'm just hoping that the new game will even the playing field."

"Same. Chris is either the luckiest man alive, or I really am that bad at strategy."

"I'm going to go with a mix of the two. We already know he's lucky. He got you." Grace grinned. "But you are surprisingly terrible at board games. I thought all your practice at reading people would have given you an edge."

I laughed. "At poker, maybe."

She fell into step behind me as we navigated our way up the narrow driveway in front of Chris's townhome and up the steps. "Thanks for inviting me again," Grace said.

"Always. I want the people who are important to me to get to know each other." I swallowed. "I… I really like him."

"I know, Mom." She pulled me into an awkward one-arm hug as she balanced the boxes under one arm. "You don't have to worry about me clinging to the dream of you and Dad getting back together. I've got a good read on how he feels about you, how both of them feel about you. I want you to know I'm really happy for you."

"I love you, sweet pea."

"Love you too." She pulled away and stepped toward the front door. "But don't think that will protect you from me kicking your butt in this game."

I chuckled as we let ourselves in. We crossed the living room into the small dining room next to the kitchen. Chris was setting up the table for a game night with soda, a few snacks like chips and dip and Red Vines, and a platter of fresh veggies for some healthy variety. I dropped the food from Slice of Life into the mix and took my seat.

Chris kissed me on the top of my head. "How was the rest of your day?"

"Good," I said. I pulled out my phone and showed him photos of the remodel. "And this room will be Bob's office."

Chris stiffened next to me and looked away.

I cocked my head to the side. "Or not?"

"I called to tell him about the Halloway case to see if it would get him to come back. I thought an active case, something to keep his mind off it, might help. But then the next one was Adrian Reynolds, and it reminded him of the scandal around his father." He hung his head. "It probably did more harm than good to tell him about it."

I rubbed his back. "He'll come back when he's ready. And until then, you are doing a fantastic job."

Grace stood with her knee braced on her chair as she unpacked the board games. "So, there's been more murders?" She kept her voice even, but with how careful she was to avoid touching the table, I could tell she didn't want me reading her emotional state.

"Yeah." I grabbed a stack of cards and started sorting them.

She nodded. "Is it something I need to be worried about?"

I wanted to shake my head, but I had promised not to lie to her about stuff. I had made a mistake similar to my grandmother's and hadn't come clean about being a witch to Grace right away. We'd both ended up stumbling through the painful transition of our divination powers manifesting alone. Hers had hit harder than mine. I was working hard on rebuilding that trust, just like she was working hard at rebuilding it with me. She'd accidentally gotten possessed by a fragment of an Outsider, and life was tense until we got it out of her. She still had nightmares about how aggressive it had made her.

"Mom?" She looked up at me.

"Not yet," I answered. "It's too soon to tell. But I'll let you know if it changes."

She nodded and continued setting up the game. Her hands moved quickly as she explained the rules. We settled in around the kitchen table with Grace on one side of me and

Chris on the other. He squeezed my knee under the table, and then we dug into the food before the first round of games began.

We'd planned for three rounds of games, but the second one went long. After a few hours of playing, the final score was Grace one, Chris one, and me in second place for both games. I was certain I would've finally claimed the title if we went again. Grace yawned as she packed things up. She gave me a quick hug before heading out. Before the door closed behind her, I made her promise not to sneak Charlie any more treats before I got home. He was an unusually large cat. He was about a year old and weighed almost twenty-five pounds. Not much of it was chunk, though. He came up to just below my knees. His size was more similar to a bobcat than a regular house cat. But I knew he wasn't one. He was a white almost ragdoll-looking cat, and he was part of a litter of kittens I'd rescued from under my porch. None of his siblings was a similar size. The only difference between him and his siblings was that he was a witch's familiar. And if the size of Gertie—Megan's familiar, which was a black-and-white cow—was any indication, witches' familiars were also a little bigger than their usual brethren. That was just unfortunate because one of his favorite things to do when I took him into work was to have me cart him around in a bag. He had recently broken another purse, and I was waiting for a heavier-duty one to arrive before I took him back in. He was displeased and demanding treats in recompense.

I followed Chris into the kitchen and helped him tidy up. The night had been fun. It reminded me of game nights my gran used to host when I was a teenager. My eyes misted.

"Thank you for making an effort with Grace," I murmured.

Chris tapped me with his hip while he did the dishes. "I knew going into this thing that you and Grace were a package deal. It would have been unreasonable to expect to date you and not get to know her too."

I bumped him back with my hip as I took up drying duties. "Not all men would feel the same way. A lot of men run when they hear the words 'single mom.'"

"She's twenty."

"I know. It's just… She's still my little girl. You know?"

He handed me another dish. "She's always going to be your daughter, but she's not little anymore. She's been through too much and fought too hard to be treated like a kid. I'm getting to know her as she is. And if becoming acquainted with another adult scares a grown man, then I don't know what to say. It seems like a weird thing to get hung up on, to me."

I fumbled with the dish and put it in the rack to dry. "I–"

"Her being part of the package deal doesn't change because she's an adult. She's important to you. She's an active part of your life. And family doesn't stop being family at eighteen." Chris swiveled toward me, put his hands on my hips and turned me around to face him. "One of the things I love most about you is how much you care about your family: blood, found, or otherwise."

My cheeks ached as my smile widened. I dropped the dishrag onto the drying rack and stepped into Chris, molding my body to his as I hugged him. "In case you didn't know, I think you're wonderful."

He wrapped his arms over my shoulders and squeezed. "Right back at you."

I still wasn't sure what I had done to deserve him. And the fact that he seemed to feel the same way baffled me. In all the years I'd been married to my ex-husband, Ed, I'd never felt so secure in my knowledge that he cherished being with me. I pulled away, and we returned to doing the dishes. We stood in a companionable silence as my mind wandered from dinner to earlier that day. My hands stilled as the image of Izzy filtered into my thoughts. She had looked so fragile.

"A penny for your thoughts?" Chris asked.

"Huh?" I blinked up at him. The dish rack was half full, and I had been drying the same plate for who knew how long. "I'm just a little distracted. Sorry."

"Are you okay?"

I shrugged. "I'm just worried about Izzy."

He continued slowly washing the dishes as he waited for me to continue.

"I haven't reached out to her in months. She looked... rough. I don't know how to describe it. I think something bad happened to her."

"It's been a rough year."

I dropped the dishrag again and spun, leaning back against the counter. "I know. But it's no excuse. I've been so wrapped up in everything going on over the last... seven months that I forgot to check in. That last case we worked together was traumatic for her, and I didn't even call to check up. I'm a bad friend."

Chris turned off the water and dried his hands. "You know that's not true. Look back at all the things you've done for your friends. You helped Heather build that cat enclosure for the Bizzy Bean. You've cleared her name, and Abby's name, from being dragged through the mud when they became people of interest in murder investigations. You let Izzy stay at your house after she found that body, no questions asked. You're a really good friend."

"But I dropped the ball. I forgot to reach out. She needed something, and I—"

He pulled me into a tight hug, capturing my hands against his chest. He rested his head on the top of mine. "You're a witch. Last I checked, witches are still human. And humans can only handle so much before one of the many plates, or balls, or whatever you want to call it, falls. It doesn't make you a bad person. Or even a bad friend. It makes you human. It's what you do after dropping the plate that matters. You now know she needs help. You didn't before. But you know it now. Miss Williams, you're a good person and a good friend, and you will help Izzy any way you can. Because that's what good friends do."

I relaxed into his embrace. "Maybe you're right."

"I am definitely right." He pulled back and turned the water back on. "Now, let's finish these dishes up so you can get home to Charlie before it gets too late."

CHAPTER 7

I drummed my fingers on the bottom of my steering wheel as I waited. My gaze flicked to the clock on my dash. The time was only ten minutes past two, but Izzy was rarely late—at least not the first two times we'd worked together on a case. The last time, she'd been distracted. I assumed at the time that was because she was shaken by discovering the body, but with the trend continuing, it seemed to go deeper than that. I pulled out my phone to send her a quick text when her car came into view. She parked across the street and shuffled across toward me. Her shoulders were hunched, and her hair hung limply around her face. She tucked it behind an ear as she came to a stop in front of me. I climbed out of my car to meet her.

I studied her, finding the dark bags under her eyes somehow worse. "Are you up to this? I can do it alone if you need to rest."

Izzy shook her head. "Let's just get this out of the way."

I peered at her out of the corner of my eye as we trudged across the University of Washington campus to the art building. It jutted out of the trees. The light-brown stone, with almost white gothic detailing, shone under the midday sun. It was somehow both intimidating and hopeful at the same time. The interior was much more dimly lit. My shoes squeaked against the tile flooring. Voices filtered into the halls from the classes in session. We turned into the hallway with the student studios, and the voices vanished. The air stilled, and as we approached the slightly open door to Camille's room, her emotions seeped into me.

It didn't happen often, but now and then when I was in the presence of someone who felt something with their whole being, so intensely that even those without divination powers could feel it in the air, I didn't have to touch anything to experience what they felt. With her, it was a strangely muddled feeling. I struggled around the heavy feeling in my chest as my heart clenched. Despite my erratic heartbeat, my limbs felt loose and my mouth almost cottony. When I stepped into the room, I understood.

Camille stood in the center of the room, swaying in place. She was barefoot, her big clunky Doc Marten boots kicked off into a corner. Her black skinny jeans were ripped artistically, and she wore a loose, flowing tank top over them. Every inch of exposed skin on her arms and shoulders was covered in tattoos. Her short, choppy brown hair was wild around her face. In one hand, she held a paintbrush, and in the other was a half-empty bottle of vodka. Large headphones covered her ears. She took another swig from the bottle then lunged forward with her paintbrush and attacked the canvas in front of her. Paint splattered across the blank space, which she quickly smeared into shapes. Within a few seconds, an image was forming in the paint—a figure hunched in pain.

Izzy knocked loudly on the door frame. Camille flinched and flung the paintbrush onto her workstation. She wrenched the headphones off her head and swung toward us, unsteady on her feet.

"Camille Rivera?" I asked, stepping into the room. "I… I'm a friend of Kevin's."

Camille crumpled into herself, her arms wrapping around her stomach, her shoulders hunched, and her head hung down. She squeezed her eyes closed. "He called me last night. When his name came up, I almost didn't answer because I was reading a good book. But then I realized we hadn't spoken since Christmas. Isn't it odd? Time, I mean. I don't know how nine months passed without talking to him."

"With how busy Adrian was all the time, it makes sense," Izzy said.

I shot her a quizzical look.

Izzy didn't look at me as she moved past me. Her eyes were focused on a blank spot on the wall behind Camille. "Adrian loved his brother, but you know he always preferred spending time with things that brought him joy. And after Thomas… after their dad died… it was hard finding that joy in his brother's company. But you brought it to him when he needed it most."

Camille took a faltering step forward, squinting at Izzy through her curtain of hair. "Have we met? I thought I knew all of Adrian's friends."

"I met him a handful of times."

"You knew him well for only a handful of times."

Izzy shrugged. "It was my job to read people well. I knew him well enough to know that he loved you."

Camille's face fell, and tears streaked down her face. "I always thought he loved the idea of me."

I held myself still as Izzy moved farther into the room. The grief flowing through the room had a bittersweet edge. I didn't want to break whatever rapport Izzy was building up by drawing attention to myself.

"At first, maybe. But after being around you, after really seeing you, he fell in love with the person. He… he was ring shopping." Izzy's voice cracked.

My brow furrowed. *How does she know that?* I stepped to the side to get a better view of Izzy's face and saw an earnestness in her eyes, mixed with pain. *Did she know Adrian? Why didn't she mention that yesterday? Does that mean she knew both the victims?*

Camille wiped her face. "What do you want?"

"Dani is really good at investigating." Izzy gestured toward me. "Adrian deserves the best people looking into what happened. Are you willing to talk to her about him?"

Camille nodded and turned her gaze toward me.

I swallowed as I stared into her intense hazel eyes. I could see what Adrian loved about her. Her gaze was filled with so much passion that I almost felt I was falling into her. I blinked and forced myself to focus. *What was my first question again?* I cleared my throat and latched onto the first thing to cross my mind. "Did Adrian have any enemies?"

"No." Camille frowned. "The only person he ever had issues with was his father, but he's been dead for almost a year."

"Not even one of his exes?"

"Never." A sad smile crossed her face. "You know what our second date was? One of his ex-girlfriends' weddings. I didn't know she was an ex until I got there. He forgot to mention it because by that point, they were just old friends. The situation would have been awkward if it had been anyone else. But he made it easy. Somehow, it wasn't a spite invitation. Both the bride and groom adored him. They were so happy he could be there. Being mad at him was like being mad at a golden retriever. No one could do it for long. I just can't imagine anyone getting so angry with him that they would want to kill him."

"Did he mention any arguments or disagreements in the last few days or weeks? It doesn't have to have been something big." I moved closer and took a seat on the only stool in the room.

She shook her head. "Are these sorts of questions ever helpful?"

When I opened my mouth to respond, my gaze slid behind her and landed on a painting leaning against the wall. It was a half-finished painting of a man. He was standing in the shadows, his face obscured. My skin crawled as I stared at it. The shadows were too deep. He stood at a strange angle that didn't seem natural. The words from the bookstore owner echoed in my ears: *"He moved wrong."* Glancing around, I saw it was the only piece in the room that had a foreboding aura to it. All the others, except for the one she'd started as we entered the room, were filled with hope. I stood and walked toward the painting. "What was the inspiration behind this one?"

Camille turned and cocked her head to the side. "I paint what I see."

"When did you see him?"

"A few days ago. Maybe three? He was standing on the street while I was out on a date with Adrian. He had such a strange energy about him. He caught my eye, and I couldn't get him out of my head."

I kneeled down in front of it. The paint strokes were impressionistic. It was more about the feeling he had elicited than an accurate portrayal. But I couldn't deny the wrongness of him. "It's good. Do you remember what his face looked like?"

"I only saw him for a minute before we walked into the restaurant. Enough to get an impression but not enough to sketch him in detail."

"Do you mind if I take a photo of it?" I asked.

"Is it important?" Camille moved to hover over my shoulder.

"I'm not sure yet."

"Okay." Camille stilled behind me. "You can take a picture."

I fished out my phone and snapped a few shots. I didn't know if it would be helpful or not, but I knew in my gut that he was the same guy the bookstore owner had described. My skin crawled just from looking at it. Camille really was talented. She had captured the creep factor perfectly.

I stood and stared down at my phone before shoving it into my pocket and pulling out a business card. "Thank you for your time. I am so sorry for your loss. If you think of anything, or if you see that guy again, call me." I shoved the card into her hands.

"I hope you catch whoever did this," Camille said.

We left her there with her paintings. When we exited the building, I blinked against the brightness of the sun. Izzy walked next to me in silence, her hands shoved into her pockets as we made our way back to our cars.

"Did you know Adrian?" I asked when we entered the parking garage.

Izzy flinched. "You could say that."

"It's a yes or—"

"I'm going to track down some more of his exes. You should work on whatever lead you got off that painting. And then let's regroup at the usual spot." Izzy ducked into her car.

I stepped in front of the open door before she could close it. "Are you okay?"

"I will be." Izzy turned her head away. "Just need to track down a killer. Again. Things are never boring when you're around, are they?"

"You don't have to help me," I said.

"I do, though." Izzy sighed and looked up to hold my gaze. "I'll text you when I either find something or run out of steam. Will you do the same?"

"You know you can talk to me, right?"

"Will you call me if you find something?" she repeated.

"You know I will." I stepped back. I couldn't force her to talk to me if she didn't want to.

Izzy closed her door as I took another step away from her car. She rolled her window down and gave a whisper of a smile. "Tell Heather I really like her lemon drop cookies. For when we meet back up."

I nodded and retreated to my car. I watched her as she drove away. Something was wrong with Izzy. I'd been so focused on solving the last case when she was in town that I had missed something important. I chewed on my lip as I started my car. But just like last time, I wasn't sure if I would have time to look into it right then, not with a murder investigation on my hands that involved magic. But once the case was done, if I could solve that one, I wouldn't let Izzy slip away again without getting to the bottom of it.

My magical knowledge had expanded a lot over the past year, but the case was too big for me. I texted my coven to meet me at the Bizzy Bean after closing, then I drove up to Mukilteo to take the ferry back home. One of them had to have experienced magical goop before, and if not, someone could at least give me an idea of what to do next. My only lead was a guy who felt wrong. *How am I supposed to find someone like that?*

CHAPTER 8

I claimed the last spot at my coven's booth at the Bizzy Bean. The other ladies were already gathered around it, the lights dimmed so that anyone would find it hard to see us all sitting in the back booth well past closing. Heather had her usual dusting of flour on her apron. Megan wore pajamas. Her work on her farm made her an early-to-bed-early-to-rise-type person. And the Retirees all wore their usual matching tracksuits. Their outfits were a pale yellow that day.

Despite the late hour, the cats were still out in the enclosure. They ran around the space, chasing each other in frenzied sprints. Apparently, being loved on all day had left the kittens with a serious case of the zoomies. Star, the resident foster mom cat—and mother to my Charlie—sat on her perch high over the room and watched the chaos, her eyes half closed but still tracking the movement of the little ones. Once upon a time, Charlie had been the runt of her litter, but last I checked he had at least five pounds on her. And I had the sinking suspicion he was still growing.

Heather wiped her forehead with the back of a wrist. "How's the investigating going?"

"It's gotten more complicated." I curled into myself on my

seat, my shoulders tensing before the next words left my mouth. "There was another victim yesterday."

"Who?" Betty asked.

I was half surprised she didn't already know. The Retirees had their ear to the ground and knew most of the town's gossip well ahead of me. "Adrian Reynolds."

The entire table tensed. Agnes reached down and touched the metal braid embedded into the floor. She muttered the words of her usual spells to prevent eavesdropping and to create the illusion of a much more boring conversation if anyone did try to listen in mundanely or magically. While no patrons were left in the cafe, it was still better to be safe than sorry. A Warden could always be listening in. An iridescent haze settled over the table and sank into the wood around us, making it glow gently. A nonwitch wouldn't be able to see it. And she had cast the spells in such a way that even a witch standing outside our circle wouldn't be able to pick anything up. She had gotten a lot better with her illusion magic over the past few months.

Megan leaned forward, her fingers gripping the table. "So, it's confirmed then? This has to do with Meredith?"

I grimaced and forced myself to shake my head. More and more tallies were appearing in the Meredith column, but I wouldn't go so far as to say it was certain yet. A certainty would require us to contact the Wardens, and I didn't want to risk pulling their attention unnecessarily.

"Meredith's magic was sparkly. This was goopy still. It felt different. There was the same goop at Adrian's place too. Plus, I think I might have a description of the killer."

"Really?" Sarah perked up.

I opened the photo of Camille's painting and dropped my phone in the center of the table. Betty reached for it first then handed it off to Agnes. "The bookstore owner said he saw a guy about six feet tall with dark-brown hair going into that occult shop before Delilah was killed. Adrian's girlfriend saw someone similar a few days before Adrian's death. It *feels* like they are the same person."

"Did you have any more luck looking into the past at Adrian's home?"

I slumped into my seat. "No. I didn't want to draw attention to myself with Harrison there. Plus, I'm not sure if I would have been able to do it, anyway. There was something about being there that made me nauseous."

"So, what now?" Heather asked.

I shrugged. "I was hoping one of you guys would have an idea. Have any of you heard of goopy magic before? I've never seen anything leave traces like that behind. It's always so light and airy."

Betty opened her mouth but then clamped it shut.

I sat up. "What were you about to say?"

Betty shook her head. "You wouldn't go for it anyway."

"We're brainstorming. I need all the ideas, even ones you don't think I'm going to like."

Betty crossed her arms and pursed her lips. "Why waste our time on ideas you're not going to take?"

Agnes elbowed Betty in the side. "Stop being a grump. I know checking up on Meredith's house is stressing you out, but Dani doesn't deserve your ire right now."

Betty glowered at her and dropped her arms. "Fine. Why do you always have to be right?"

"Because I'm wonderful like that," Agnes said.

Betty straightened in her seat. "It's not a new suggestion. Sarah made it already, and I think she's right. No offense, but Grace is better at looking into the past than you are. You should take her to one of the crime scenes and have her take a crack at it."

My stomach tightened. Betty was right. While I could have prophetic dreams of the future, Grace was much better at looking backward than me. *But she's my daughter. It's my job to keep her safe.* I shook my head. "She's still recovering."

Megan reached out and touched my arm. "Have you asked her if she's still recovering?"

"She's my daughter. I know her. I couldn't… She deserves some peace after everything she's been through."

Betty's expression softened. "I'm not saying throw her into the deep end. But we're cursed. There is no peace for any of us."

"And she would be the first to tell you she isn't a child anymore," Sarah said.

A sour taste formed at the back of my throat as my limbs became heavy. I tilted my head back, resting it against the booth. *Maybe they're right. Grace is my baby. A twenty-year-old baby. She can make her own decisions on this.* "Fine. I'll ask her." Before I could talk myself out of it, I grabbed my phone from the table.

DANI:
Hey, sweetie. I'm investigating again, and there is something you might be able to help me with.

GRACE:
I'll do it.

DANI:
I haven't told you what it is yet.

GRACE:
And? I'll still do it.

DANI:
Meet me at Madame Halloway's.

I texted her the address and stood. "Alright, let's go ask my daughter to witness a murder."

I was being dramatic, but I couldn't help it. In all the times I'd looked into the past, I hadn't seen any of the acts of violence in any detail. The things I saw were more like glimpses of things that could be useful. I had no reason to think it would be different for Grace. But that didn't make me feel any better about asking her to risk seeing something violent.

Fifteen minutes later, we were all gathered outside Madam Halloway's occult shop. The neon sign had been turned off, and police tape covered the door. I shifted my weight between my feet, staring at it. I'd already been inside. I knew forensics had cleared the place. Chris wouldn't mind if I went back in. But I wasn't sure how he would feel about all of us traipsing through the place.

"Are you ready?" Megan murmured next to me.

My muscles tightened, but I nodded anyway.

Agnes stepped away from the group and joined hands with Megan to cast a spell over the group, to create an illusion of us all standing around chatting on the sidewalk. It wouldn't hold for long. Betty scuttled forward and worked at the lock. Over the years, she'd had a wide range of jobs, from working at a mechanic's shop to being a locksmith one summer. While she was rusty, she knew how to get around simple door locks with ease. She took only thirty seconds to pick the lock and push the door inward. She backed away enough so that Grace and I could dip inside before the illusion failed.

At night, the interior of the shop was disconcerting. The shelves loomed over us, and the shadows were so deep that I couldn't see into all the corners of the room.

Grace choked back a gasp next to me. "What is that?"

"It feels wrong in here, doesn't it?"

She made a sound of agreement next to me and took a jerky step forward into the room. "Let's be quick about this, then."

I guided her to the painting on the far wall. It was the only object in the room with the necessary eyes to look into the past. Grace held her hand up, her fingers hovering over the woman's face, and muttered the words to the spell she needed. Purple sparkles sputtered out of her mouth. They swayed in the air, floating slowly toward the painting. Her fingers brushed against the woman's eyes as the sparkles sank into her fingertips. Her breath hitched, then she gagged. She yanked her hand back to cover her mouth.

"Shoot," Grace said.

"It's okay. Just try again."

She shook her head. "The spell landed. I saw about two seconds before I felt like I was going to hurl my guts up. I'm sorry, Mom."

An object could only be used once as a focus for a spell like that. We wouldn't be able to try again with the painting. I chewed on my lip. I'd brought my witch's kit, which had an obsidian mirror. It was in my car, so I would just have to duck outside to get it. With it, we could try to force our divination powers to give us a vision. At places where something terrible had happened, it always looked backward toward that. But that was different from the spell that let you access the senses of an object. It overtook your senses completely. With it, I had experienced the moment of someone's death before. I didn't want that for Grace.

"It's okay. I'll figure something else out."

Grace shook her head and pulled something out from her own pocket. "I'll try something else."

My breath caught as I recognized the object in her hand. It was a twin to my own obsidian mirror.

"You don't have to—"

"I want to." Grace lifted the mirror in front of her face. Her hands shook as she stared into the black surface.

I reached out and twined my fingers through hers. She was as stubborn as me. I couldn't have talked her out of it. But that didn't mean she had to do it alone. I steadied my breathing and exhaled motes of light. They were more sluggish than usual as nausea rolled through me. I breathed steadily in through my nose and out through my mouth and focused on forming the motes of light into a stream that flowed down into my hand and into Grace. She squeezed my fingers and muttered the words to the next spell. Her purple sparkles came out stronger and seemed more sure of themselves. They flowed easily from her mouth to the mirror in her hand.

Grace moved slowly through the room. I followed her, willing more and more of my magic into her as she maintained the spell. She came to a stop a few inches from where Delilah had been killed. Her hand shook in mine. She gagged and yanked her hand away from me as she retched. She covered her mouth at the last second and dashed for the door. She made it two feet out the door before she lost her dinner.

"Are you okay?" I asked.

Grace was bent over, her hands on her knees, her hair held back from her face by Agnes. She held a hand out toward me. "Get me my sketchbook. I saw his tattoo."

CHAPTER 9

I dashed away from my coven clustered on the sidewalk and unlocked Grace's car. It was messier than mine, with a pile of discarded clothes in the back seat, intermixed with crumpled receipts and books. At least she didn't eat in her car. I dove into the front seat and grabbed her backpack from the floor. Her sketchbook was in the second pocket I checked. I fished out a box of charcoal pencils and felt-tip pens and sprinted back to where Grace was sitting slumped against the building. I handed it to her and flopped down onto the still-warm concrete next to her.

Grace's hand still trembled as she flipped to a blank page. As she drew, her movements became steadier.

"Can you describe what you saw?" Betty asked.

Grace furrowed her brow and grabbed a fine-tipped pen from the box. "It was discombobulated. I could tell it was a man with dark hair. There was something wrong with him. I think he was sick. His skin was... gray? Whenever I tried to look at his face, the nausea got worse, so I tried to focus on his other features. He was wearing a white shirt. It was like one of those undershirts men like to wear under button-ups. He had a tattoo on his forearm. I really tried to look at his face, but it made me vomit. Sorry I couldn't be more helpful."

I squeezed her shoulder. "You were very helpful."

She gave me a weak smile and thrust the sketchbook into my hands. That tattoo was of a woman with angel wings. The proportions were strange. The woman's face was much too big for her body, her eyes almost wide and cartoonish, but the wings were soft and delicate with fine lines. Despite her too-big eyes, she was oddly beautiful, with a fierce expression on her face. Her hands were balled into fists, and her chin jutted out as if in a dare. I had never seen anything quite like it before.

"Maybe you should ask a local tattoo artist if they recognize it. It seems pretty distinctive," Agnes said.

I grabbed my phone and took a quick photo of the art then searched for local tattoo shops. A block away, there was one closing in seventeen minutes.

"Could you guys make sure Grace gets home okay?" I asked. "I've got a tattoo artist to interview."

Sarah nodded. "I'll drive her car back. Betty can swing by to pick me up when she's done doing the evening check of Meredith's house."

"Thank you." I pulled each of the women in turn into a quick hug. I squeezed Grace's shoulder then turned to sprint down the street. While the website said they closed at nine, I didn't want to risk missing them.

I skidded to a stop outside the shop. The lights were still on, and the Open sign hung over the door. I pushed it open and stepped inside. I hadn't been in a place like that since Grace was sixteen and wanted to get an industrial bar piercing at the top of her left ear. That hadn't lasted long. It kept getting caught on things, so she eventually took it out. But I had insisted on getting it done there versus at one of those kiosks at the mall. Statistically it was much safer.

The shop was small, with only one workstation at the

back. A half-folded privacy screen hid most of it. The main waiting area had a single couch and chair that faced each other over a coffee table overflowing with books of art. As the bell jingled when the door closed behind me, a man stood up from behind the screen. He was one of the tallest people I'd ever seen. He stood a good head above the privacy screen, his hair only a few inches from the ceiling. It was a dark brown, shorter on the sides than on the top, and it curled down over his forehead. A silver hoop nose ring caught the light as he shifted around the screen. Once he came into full view, he was even more impressive, with wide shoulders and ink covering him from the tips of his fingers all the way to his chin. The only part of him not covered in tattoos was his face.

"We'll be closing soon, but I have a small window in the morning if you were looking for something quick." His voice was surprising. It was soft and wrapped around me like a warm blanket.

"I'm not looking to get a tattoo, sorry."

"A piercing, then?" He cocked his eyebrow.

I shook my head and handed him the sketchbook. "I was hoping you might recognize some work."

He glanced down at it. "What's this for?"

"I'm not sure if you've heard, but there was a murder down the street."

He grunted. "Delilah. I did her back piece a few years back."

"Someone saw a person coming out of her shop the morning of, who had that tattoo on his forearm."

I studied his face as I spoke. His expression was pensive, his brow furrowed, and the tip of his tongue stuck out the corner of his mouth in concentration.

"I wanted to ask him some questions."

"Definitely not my style, but I recognize whose it is. She

used to have a shop around here. It's not often that you see fine-line black and gray mixed with New School like this."

"Where is she now?"

"New York. She moved out East a few years back."

I deflated as he handed the sketchbook back to me. I shoved it into my purse.

"But you're in luck," he said.

My head snapped back up.

"Nova's going to be in town in two days for a convention in Seattle. She's flying in and out same day for this massive charity fundraiser. Let me write her information down for you." He retreated behind the privacy screen and returned a minute later with a piece of paper. "Her name's Nova Cross. She won't have much time to chat, but if you're willing to sit for a quick flash piece or find someone who doesn't mind you hovering over them while she works, you should be able to get a few questions in. I would bet she remembers this one. She's got a mind like a steel trap."

I swallowed as I stared down at the note in my hand. *A quick flash piece?* I had considered getting a tattoo before, but I could never settle on a design. My stomach dropped at the idea of getting something so permanent for the sake of the investigation. *I sure hope I can find someone who doesn't mind me hovering.* I held up the piece of paper. "Thank you, Mister…?"

"Briggs." He held his hand out to shake. "Talon Briggs. Tell Nova I sent you. We've got a good rapport."

"Thanks." I shook his hand then backed out of the store.

The sun had set over an hour before. The street was finally beginning to cool. I strolled back to my car, my mind going a mile a minute as I turned over everything I knew in my head. I had a lot more questions than answers. The killer was a guy who looked unwell. Men couldn't use magic, but magic was involved. *Maybe he has an enchanted item at his disposal? I've seen those before. If so, what's its effect? Is it making him sick? And how does Izzy know both of the victims?* I hoped Nova Cross would remember him and could give me a name.

I drove back home with the radio on, but I couldn't focus on the music. Before I knew it, I was parked outside my house. Grace's bedroom light was on. I trudged into the house. Charlie stood at the top of the stairs. He meowed softly at me as I entered. I chucked off my shoes and padded up the stairs to him. I grunted as I picked him up. He wrapped his paws around my shoulder and nestled his head under my ear, purring.

"I missed you too, buddy."

He happily pawed at my shoulder as I carried him to bed. I discarded my purse on my nightstand and curled around Charlie. It wasn't even ten yet, but my day had been exhausting. I drifted off to sleep with questions rattling around in my head. *Did Delilah and Adrian know each other? Why these two?*

CHAPTER 10

I felt ice inside me. It was so cold that it almost felt hot. My clothes were wet and clung to my body. I lurched forward, my legs not bending right under me. The floor swayed, shifting from side to side. I was staring at a door. I tried to force myself to look to the side, but my head wouldn't move. *What's going on?* I took another lurching step forward. Something heavy was in my hand. It dragged along the floor behind me. Seagulls cawed in the distance as the floor rocked harder under me—not a floor but a deck. *How did I get on a boat?*

I reached out and pulled on the door handle. My skin was a sickly gray, and wrapped around my forearm was an angel wing. *Holy moly.* I'd had prophetic dreams from the perspective of the victim before, but never the killer. *Where am I? Whose boat is this?* I focused on as many details as I could. The deck was a lighter wood, teak maybe. Out of the corner of my eye, I could make out a white sail. The door was somewhat unique. It was hand carved, with the image of a moon hanging low over the water, in the center. The wood was painted a dark blue that faded to black at the edges, and the moon was a soft white with patches of gray in the center.

The door opened easily under my hand, and I staggered downstairs. The space below was a single room. It was cozy. The moon theme from the door above had been carried into the space. The decorations were dark colors with soft white accents. A bed was built into the far wall. Across from it was a small kitchen galley with a single door that led off to a bathroom sitting in between. A man was standing in the kitchen. He turned as I reached the bottom of the stairs. He wore jeans over work boots and a worn T-shirt with a faded band logo in the center. His hair was shaggy and hung in loose curls around his ears.

The man met my gaze, and his expression shifted from surprise to shock to horror as his mouth opened. "You're—"

I had been lumbering across the room as I studied his face. My hand rose behind me, and I struck, cutting off his words as a tire iron came down on him.

I jerked awake in bed, a scream ripping its way out of my throat. The room was dark. It had been daytime in the vision. I still had time. *I can stop it.* I scrambled out of bed and grabbed Grace's sketchbook from the nightstand. I turned on the lights and fumbled with the pencils. I sketched out a very rough outline of the man's face. The proportions weren't right. I flipped the page and started again. I had taken a few art classes in high school and one in college. I hadn't kept up with it at all. While I was great at photography, drawing had never been my strong suit. Try as I might, I couldn't get what was in my head onto the page. After three more attempts, I threw the sketchbook down on the bed and paced the room.

Charlie moved from next to my pillow to the foot of my bed. He stared at me as I walked.

A soft knock at the door stopped me in my tracks. "Are you alright in there?" Grace asked from the hallway, her voice muffled.

"I had a bad dream," I said.

"A bad dream or a *bad* dream?"

"The latter."

My bedroom door opened a crack, and Grace peered inside. She pushed the door open the rest of the way and stepped into the room. "Can I help?"

I pinched the bridge of my nose. "Probably not. Unless you know a way to draw something I dreamed about."

"I might," she said.

I dropped my hand. I hadn't been entirely serious when I threw out that suggestion. As far as I knew, nobody could draw someone else's dream. And if she knew how to do it, I wasn't sure if I wanted her to, not after what I'd asked her to witness at Madam Halloway's. "It's okay, sweetie. I'm sure I'll figure something out."

One corner of Grace's mouth quirked up. "Are you doing that thing where you try to protect me from experiencing bad things again?"

"Maybe?"

"We live in the same house. There's no way for me not to feel it."

I grimaced. While I struggled under the weight of trying to stop bad things from happening, she had to live with the pain of witnessing it all. Neither one of us could turn it off. "That doesn't mean you have to see it too."

"Better to see it now than to see it later and also feel your guilt over a perceived failure."

"It would be—"

She raised her eyebrows and crossed her arms over her chest. We had talked many times over the past few months about the fact that even if something felt like my responsibility, that didn't mean it was my responsibility. But knowing that intellectually didn't stop the feeling. I knew that man was going to die. *What type of person would I be if I didn't at least try to do something?*

"By your logic, isn't it my responsibility to help you?" she asked.

I glowered at her. "When did you become so wise?"

She shrugged and crossed the room. "I learned from the best." She stopped next to my pillow and stared at it.

"What are you doing?"

"I've been working with Agnes on dream magic. I'm checking to see if there is any residual dream energy on your pillow."

I stepped up next to her and scooped Charlie up into my arms. I studied her as she looked down at my pillow. Her eyes were relaxed, like she wasn't looking at the pillow but past it.

"I didn't know you were working with Agnes on dream magic. When did that start?" I asked.

"About four months ago. The nightmares weren't going away, and she offered to help."

I swallowed. Grace hadn't slept well for weeks after she was freed from her Outsider possession. It had made her do things and had filled her with so much vitriol that she couldn't get it out of her head. She finally started to settle a few weeks back. I thought the memories were fading. I sighed and tried not to reprimand myself too hard for missing something else. I had been too focused on trying to find any sign that the Outsider had escaped or that Meredith was back to see all the work Grace was putting in behind the scenes. I didn't know how to pay attention to everything. No matter what I did, I would drop something in my overly ambitious attempt to juggle it all.

"Gotcha." Grace leaned forward and muttered the words to a spell I didn't recognize. Purple sparkles danced out of her mouth. They twirled in a mesmerizing pattern over my pillow until they created a blanket of light. Grace lowered her hand until it was bathed in the warm glow of her magic and pushed down. The purple mesh lowered with her hand until it sank into the pillowcase. Grace's breath hitched in her throat, and the glow over the pillow case faded. She picked up her hand and shook it out before reaching toward me. "Sketchbook?"

I shifted Charlie higher on my chest and balanced him on one arm as I retrieved the sketchbook from the tangle of blankets at the foot of the bed. I held it out for her. She took it and retreated to the chair. She flopped down and pulled her legs up after her to sit cross-legged in the seat. My arms complained about Charlie's weight, so I sank down to the floor so that I could lower him to my lap without losing contact. He purred the lingering unease from my dream away as I stroked his head behind his ears.

Grace sat hunched in the chair, her eyes focused on the page in front of her as she drew. "So, what do you want to know about dream magic?"

"I had planned on waiting to ask questions until you were done."

"I can feel your curiosity from here." Grace grabbed another pencil from the case on the nightstand. "I'm only a novice, so I can only really tell you about the two things I've learned how to do."

"Okay." I shifted into a more comfortable position, making Charlie chirp in protest of his seat moving under him. "What are the two things you've learned how to do?"

"I can prevent myself from dreaming, which isn't ideal in the long run. We need to dream to process things. It makes sleep a whole lot less restful. And I can also relive a dream if there is still dream residue on my pillow. Dream residue is sort of like the emotional residue people leave behind when they touch an object. Except for instead of lingering on in perpetuity like emotions do, it fades quickly."

I scrunched up my nose. "Why on earth would you want to relive a nightmare?"

"They were always the same. But it was hard to recognize that while I was in it. By taking a step back, I could identify moments in the dream where it would be easier to figure out

I was dreaming. And once I knew I was dreaming, I could take control of it—at least, in theory. I'm still working on that second part. It's still a bit hit or miss although I'm successful more often than not these days."

I continued to scratch Charlie behind his ears. A new thought was worming its way into my head, and I didn't like it. If I didn't voice it, though, it would fester. I sighed. "Why didn't you tell me about this?" *Why didn't you want me to help?*

"I'm too much like you, I guess." She stood and handed me the sketchbook. "I didn't want you to worry."

I tucked some hair behind her ear. "It's my job to worry."

"I didn't mean to hide it from you. I just... I could feel how scared you were. I didn't want to make it worse. I wish I could say that was just for you, but I was being selfish too. I didn't want to feel how anxious you were all the time. I'm sorry."

My emotions warred inside of me. I clamped them down and tried to find a calm place inside myself. The last thing she needed was for me to emotionally bleed all over her. *I really should take up meditation. Or yoga. Isn't that supposed to center your thoughts or something?* I forced a smile onto my face. Even if she knew I wasn't happy, she could at least know I was trying.

"It's okay. I love you, and I know you need to take care of yourself. So long as you're reaching out to someone in my coven for help with these things... then I'll be happy."

Grace nodded and slunk back to the door. She turned her head toward me before she slipped out into the hallway. "Goodnight, Mom. I love you too."

"Thank you for the help," I said before the door closed.

I stared down at the face of the man in my dreams. It wasn't perfect, but it was a whole lot better than I could ever do. The shape of his features was right. She had tried to shift it to a more neutral expression instead of one of shock or horror. He looked almost placid. It was a good likeness, though. If he had a boat, that meant he had to dock it somewhere. Someone at one of the local marinas would recognize him. I dropped the sketchbook back onto the nightstand and climbed back into bed. Charlie snuggled down into his usual spot and placed a paw on my shoulder as if to tell me everything was going to be okay.

CHAPTER 11

The headache that had formed behind my eyes midmorning hadn't gone away. I'd spent all day frantically driving from home inspections for my day job as an independent property claims adjuster to the various marinas around Whidbey Island. At each one so far, no one had recognized the drawing of the man from my dream. The Puget Sound was huge. I didn't want to think about the possibility that he'd moored his boat off another island. I was quickly losing hope, though. I'd already checked all the larger facilities and had moved onto a few smaller private docks that housed only a few boats. At my seventh stop of the day, I was quickly running out of time before I had to meet Heather and Izzy at the Bizzy Bean for a case update. I was hoping to bring something concrete, but if my luck kept going in the same direction, all I would have for all my work was the drawing of a tattoo.

I parked across the street from the dock. It wasn't large, with space for about eight boats total, and half of them were missing. I strode down the walkway, sliding my eyes from boat to boat, hoping to find at least one of the remaining four still occupied. At the final boat, I paused at the sound of someone cursing. A head popped up from behind the rail, red-faced and puffing. She wiped a hand covered in a thick plastic glove across her forehead, then she ducked back down.

"Everything all right up there?" I asked.

The woman scrambled to her feet. Her long brown hair was tied into a messy bun at the back of her neck. She wore overalls that had paint stains splattered across them, with a black tank top underneath. "Yes. Hi. Everything's fine. I'm repainting, and one of my dang kids knocked over one of the cans. It looks like a murder scene up here. Well, if blood were hot pink and not, like, red. I'm also not sure where all the glitter came from. I'm blathering. Sorry. You're the first adult I've spoken to all week. Where are my manners? Hi. I'm Carol. I don't normally word vomit at people. Can I help you with something?"

I remembered that stage of parenthood. When Grace was around five or six and got into literally everything, I gushed way too much every Monday morning when I got into work and got to speak to someone who communicated in full sentences that didn't randomly segue into nonsensical stories.

"Yeah. I'm looking for someone. Permission to come aboard to ask a few questions?"

"Sure, although I can't promise the glitter won't attack you," she said.

I grabbed the edge of the railing and kicked my legs out and over it as I hoisted myself up. I slid onto the deck a few inches from the paint splatter. The poor woman hadn't been joking when she said it looked like a murder scene. Bright-pink paint was splattered everywhere. Glitter clung in spots as if someone had danced through it, throwing handfuls of the stuff up into the air. Based on the tiny footprints that skipped through the mess, I probably wasn't far off in my mental image. She had been overly generous in claiming one of her kids had knocked it over. What had happened was more than that. The scene was gleeful chaos.

Carol flushed as I took in the mess. "Who are you looking for?"

I pulled out the sketchbook and flipped to the right page. I held it out for her to look at. "I don't have a name, just a physical description. He looks sort of like this."

"Ah. He's Moonlight Whisper."

"Moonlight Whisper?" I cocked an eyebrow.

She ducked her head and pointed at one of the empty spots across the way. "He rents that space over there. I never actually caught the guy's name. He mostly keeps to himself. But his sailboat is named Moonlight Whisper. It's a piece of art." Her eyes took on a faraway look as a smile ghosted her lips. "The woodwork. The paint detailing. He sure knows how to work with his hands. I've always wanted to get a closer look at it. He's beautiful. I mean the boat is beautiful."

I tucked the drawing away. "Do you know when he'll be back?"

"Maybe later today? Or sometime tomorrow? He left this morning, and he's not usually gone for more than a day or two."

"Thanks." I grabbed one of my business cards from its holder. "When he comes back, could you let him know I was looking for him?"

She took my card and slipped it into a pocket. She waved as I disembarked and made my way back up the dock. I hadn't handled any claims for boats out there, so I wasn't sure how easy it would be to find an owner's name based on a ship's name. I mentally added it to the list of things I still needed to research as I got into my car and drove the thirty minutes back to Point Pleasant.

Izzy was already at a table when I arrived at the Bizzy Bean. She had claimed a spot in the middle of the cat enclosure. One of the newest kittens was curled up in the crook of her arm, receiving head scratches while she waited. I caught Heather's eye and cocked my head toward the enclosure. She held up her finger, whispered something to Becca, one of her usual baristas, and slipped out to join me with a plate of cookies in hand. Side by side, we strode up to the table and claimed the two remaining seats around it.

Heather slid the plate of cookies to the center. They were lemon-drop cookies with a white glaze drizzled over the top. "It looks like the three musketeers are back together to solve another case."

Izzy grabbed a cookie from the plate. "Does that mean we're still waiting for our own D'Artagnan to show up?"

I chuckled. I had never read the book, but I had enjoyed the movie, growing up. While the Three Musketeers hadn't led boring lives, things did get a lot more lively after D'Artagnan arrived.

"I sure hope not. We get into enough trouble as it is." I grabbed a cookie from the plate myself and took a bite. It was perfectly sweet and tangy. I stiffed a groan as I chewed. "Have you found anything interesting yet? Or did you run out of steam?"

Izzy grumbled as she broke her cookie in two. "Out of steam. I asked around about Adrian's exes, and everything Camille said about them seems to be right. While there's a long string of them, none of them were upset about being his ex. They all somehow ended on good terms. They were still friends. And all of them seemed truly heartbroken that he was gone. It's honestly bizarre. I thought anyone past thirty who was still a bachelor would have at least one jilted lover out there."

"Shoot, I was hoping you would have something more concrete."

"I take it your mysterious lead from the painting hasn't turned anything up?" Izzy asked.

I glanced over at Heather. "I found a few things. But nothing solid yet."

Izzy polished off her first cookie and grabbed a second. The dark circles hadn't gotten any better under her eyes, but her energy seemed a little bit better that day. By the look of the large empty coffee cup sitting next to her, I was willing to bet that had more to do with an abundance of caffeine and sugar than a good night's sleep.

I pulled out the sketchpad and flipped it open to the page with the tattoo. "I showed it around. It jogged the memory of one of the witnesses. They remembered seeing a guy come out of Madam Halloway's with a tattoo that looked like this on his forearm."

Izzy pulled the sketchpad toward her. "Which witness?"

"Oh gosh, I didn't catch his name." I fumbled for a response. I wanted to say the bookstore owner, but she might double-check my work. "He was at one of the local businesses?" *Better to keep it vague.*

My heartbeat quickened slightly as she handed it back to me. While her face remained blank, her skepticism was obvious in the emotions that lingered on the page.

"What now?" Heather asked.

"The tattoo artist who did this is at a convention in Seattle today." I held Izzy's gaze. "You up to getting a tattoo done in the name of justice?"

"Yeah. Lead the way."

I did a double take. She'd said yes immediately. I studied her, trying to figure out where she might have some hidden ink. I had never noticed a tattoo on her before.

She caught me staring and leaned back to pull up a corner of her sweatshirt. The tattoo started just above her hip and wrapped upward along her side, hugging her curves. It was of a cherry blossom tree with flower petals drifting down. Hidden inside the branches of the tree was a bird. I couldn't make out what type. Its head disappeared under the edge of her shirt. "It's my biggest piece. I've also got this one." She twisted in her seat and lifted her hair, revealing a small origami crane holding a quill on the nape of her neck. It was normally hidden by her hair. "And this one." She rolled up the sleeve of her left arm. Scrolled in a neat, flowery script were the words *Ink is the voice of the unheard.* "I also have some morse code on my ankle and moons going down my spine."

"They're beautiful," I said. The details on the tree and origami crane were breathtaking. They were all artistically done. I smiled at Izzy.

I quickly thanked Heather for hosting again then led Izzy out to my car. Getting to where we were going would take about two hours. I hoped the tattoo artist would be able to give us a name. With Izzy at my side, the chances of having a productive outing had increased.

CHAPTER 12

After I gave Izzy a brief rundown on who we were going to see, she dozed in the front seat of the car, from the second we pulled onto the ferry headed to Mukilteo until the second I parked in an underground garage a few blocks from the convention center. With the overcast sky and the skyscrapers looming over the street, the air was almost cool at ground level. I was glad of that. The steep hills made my legs burn as I hiked up the steep hills to Pike.

Izzy trailed after me as we made our way into the convention hall. I bought a pass in the registration room and pushed my way through the doors into the main hall. The sudden onslaught of noise made my ears ring. My vision tunneled as my gaze bounced around the room. A sea of people surged in and out of the rows of booths, each booth housing a single tattoo artist. I swallowed, trying to bring moisture to my mouth. Finding the right person was going to be harder than I thought. *I can do this. Don't panic.* I squared my shoulders and marched to the first row of booths. I had looked at the convention's website online, and only one Nova Cross had a booth there. As long as she had her name posted somewhere, I would find her.

"I'll read the names on the right if you take the left," I suggested.

Izzy nodded, and we walked down the rows together, side by side. Seven rows—and more tattoo artists than I could easily count—later, I found her. She had a small crowd around her table. They were clustered so tightly around the booth that I couldn't see her behind the swarm of people. I grabbed Izzy's hand and shoved my way through until I found what looked like a line.

"What's this?" I asked a guy wearing a motorcycle jacket over leather pants beside me, gesturing toward the line.

"They're all waiting to get work done."

"Do we take a number or...?"

He snorted. "She's booked out. Those are the ones who got here early enough to get on her schedule. We're all just camping out, hoping she has enough time to fit one more in."

My jaw dropped. Talon had mentioned she was tattooing for charity. I hadn't realized she would be quite so popular. I chewed on my lip as I studied the line, my gaze flicking from person to person then over to the artist. Nova Cross was interesting to look at. She wore massive combat boots that added a good six inches to her height. Even with them, she wasn't much past five feet. Her hair was a bright teal with lilac highlights. She had it up in space buns. To complete her look, she had on a short plaid miniskirt and a white crop top that buttoned up the center, with a red tie loose around her neck. Every inch of skin on her arms, legs and exposed midriff were covered in black and gray tattoos that had a vague floral design.

Her customers were a mix, from people dressed like Nova to a woman who looked like a soccer mom. Standing between them and her was a gangly teenager directing the line like he was directing traffic. Despite the noise and the push of bodies, he looked at ease as he yelled at people to get back in their places and to stop sitting.

"What now?" Izzy whispered.

"I don't know. Convince one of the people to let us talk to Nova while she works or... hope someone drops out and we're lucky enough to snag their spot?"

Nova was wrapping the arm of her current customer in some sort of clear wrap and giving care instructions as the traffic director called on the next person in line. I slipped in closer as the traffic guy quickly cut a piece of paper out of a stack and handed it to the latest client.

"Give this to Nova and tell her where you want it. No ribs, no neck, and no armpits. Got it?" Traffic Guy said.

The client nodded and strode past.

Before they got too far away to hear, I reached out. "Excuse me, do you mind if we watch?"

The customer shrugged me off. "You can see perfectly fine from back there."

I gritted my teeth and stepped back into the crowd next to Izzy.

"No luck?" Izzy asked.

I shook my head.

"Let me see if any of the other ones are going to be more friendly." Izzy sidled up the line and began to chat.

I looked between Nova and the rest of the line. While she was moving quickly, getting through all those people would take her hours. *What if the only person who says yes is the second to last person, and she runs out of time before she gets to them?* I studied the next person to try to get a read on her. She bounced from foot to foot with a very large iced coffee clutched between her hands. I smiled. While convincing someone who didn't know us to let us watch might be hard, I could nudge it in the right direction easily enough.

I murmured the words to the spell that would turn her iced coffee into a relaxation potion. Motes of light shot out of my mouth toward the cup. But when the spell was half out of my mouth, someone jostled me from behind. The words became garbled in my mouth, and I lost focus for half a second. My intention shifted from calming to anxious as I watched the motes dip and dive in the space between us. The lights settled over the coffee, and it flashed a golden color before a glow settled over it. The glow was sharper than normal and pulsed strangely as she lifted the drink back up to her lips.

The woman's eyes bulged out, and she hopped even more animatedly from foot to foot. As the guy directing traffic called her forward to select a design, she dropped her drink and turned on her heel. She darted into the crowd, rushing for the bathroom.

"Ma'am?" the guy bellowed after her. His voice was surprisingly deep.

Izzy darted after her. Over the sea of voices, I couldn't hear what she said, but whatever it was did the trick. The woman shoved her ticket into Izzy's waiting hands, then she was running away through the crowd, her face ashen.

Nova jumped up from her stool and stretched out her arms. "Who's next?"

"Me!" Izzy held up the ticket as she walked back to the line. She handed it to the bouncer and flipped through the options.

While Izzy selected her piece, I inched forward. "Miss Cross? If you have a minute, could you look at something for me?"

The gangly kid stepped between us and crossed his arms.

"She's with me," Izzy said.

The kid stepped back and reclaimed his position as the line's gatekeeper.

Izzy plopped down in the chair and pulled her arm out of her sweater, revealing her left shoulder. "I was thinking about here. What do you think, Dani?"

I took up a place next to Izzy and nodded. Nova got straight to work. She placed a piece of paper over Izzy's arm and wetted it until the design transferred from the page to Izzy's skin. It was an octopus climbing out of a diamond frame. The lines were simple and flowing.

"You two together?" Nova asked.

"We are." I fished the sketchbook out of my bag. "Talon Briggs said you might be able to help me," I said.

Nova looked up, her hand paused midmotion, reaching for her tattoo gun. "Talon? How's that old fart doing?"

I fumbled with the sketch pad and almost dropped it as I held it out toward her. "He's good."

She grabbed the sketch pad and started flipping through it. "You've got some real talent."

"I—"

"Although I'm assuming you wanted to ask me about my piece you drew instead of all these drawings of a creepy lady?"

I winced. Half of Grace's sketchbook was filled with her drawings of Meredith. She looked wrathful in all of them. "You recognize it, then?"

"Of course." She handed the sketch pad back. "It was my first custom piece."

"Do you remember who you did it on?"

She shook her head as she got back to work. "There were, like, eight of them—all high school friends who were joining the military after graduation. I remember one of them was a bit of an artist themselves although I think he painted. Another was a math nerd. Never did figure out how he ended up in that friend group. And another was some sort of football star for the Point Pleasant High team."

"When was that?"

"Summer of 2002." She stuck her tongue out of one corner of her mouth in concentration as she inked another line.

I shoved the notebook back into my bag. There couldn't have been that many football stars from that year. Point

Pleasant High wasn't a big school. Their graduating classes usually had two hundred students at most. An athlete like that would stand out. I backed away from the table to give Nova more space to work. About thirty minutes later, Izzy's left bicep was wrapped in clear plastic.

She was silent as she followed me out of the convention. She didn't speak until we were halfway down the block to the car. "Sounds like a decent lead. What's next?"

"It's another thread to pull on, at least. You in the mood for pie?"

If anyone would have pictures of the football team from 2001, it would be Willow Hargrave, the owner of the Slice of Life Diner. She collected photos and memorabilia of the town's history. The impacts of 9/11 had rippled throughout the country. She would definitely have a ton of photos from that time. When I pulled out my phone to check on traffic, a message popped up on my screen.

> **CHRIS:**
> There's been another murder.

CHAPTER 13

I met Chris at the Point Pleasant ferry terminal. In early afternoon, the midday rush had subsided. Izzy trailed behind me as I strode toward him. I offered to drop her off at the Bizzy Bean and come back, but she refused to be left behind. I only hoped that Chris didn't mind a surprise guest joining us as he sneaked me into a crime scene. He looked at her as I walked up. For half a second, his eyebrows rose, but then he schooled his expression and gave me a reassuring smile.

"Where to?" I asked.

Chris grabbed my hand and twined his fingers through mine as he turned and walked away from the terminal. "It's close by. The coast guard towed it in this morning."

My stomach dropped. *Am I too late? How likely is it that there would be a second murder on a boat?* I gripped his hand to keep mine from shaking.

Chris cleared his throat and squeezed my hand back. "Forensics has already cleared the scene, so you can get on board. Don't move anything unnecessarily, just in case they do need to come back for something, okay?"

"Roger that," Izzy said.

My mouth went dry as we walked toward the boat,

moored at the small marina next to the terminal. The hull was painted white, and in dark-blue navy paint were the words Moonlight Whisper. I squeezed his hand harder. That was the ship from my dream. I had failed. I had no doubt in my mind. I hadn't tracked him down quickly enough.

"What was his name?" I whispered.

Chris glanced down at me. "Vincent Callahan."

I angled my body toward him to hide what I was doing from Izzy as I pulled out the sketchbook from my purse. I showed him the drawing Grace had done of the man from my dream. "Is this him?"

Chris nodded.

I closed my eyes and slipped it back into my bag. He had already set sail that morning. I had gone as fast as I could. I faltered. "The coast guard towed it in?"

"A few hours ago. It was found around noon, floating in the bay. It almost hit another boat. When no one responded to hails, they contacted the coast guard. Looks like whoever did it swam aboard from another vessel and clocked him over the head."

My eyes widened. *How am I supposed to stop something like that? It's too much.* I pushed the negative thoughts aside. "Okay. Let's take a look."

I followed Chris up onto the boat. As my feet hit the deck, I was overcome with both a sense of déjà vu and the nausea of the lingering magic on the deck. I followed the path the killer had walked toward the handcrafted wooden door. My feet were heavy as I trudged down the short flight of stairs into the belly of the boat. Vincent hadn't put up much of a fight. The chair had been knocked over, and that was it. If not for the dark stain in the middle of the floor and the coppery scent that hung in the air, the scene would have looked peaceful. I swallowed as bile threatened the back of my throat. It could have looked peaceful, but even without those few signs, the feeling of wrongness would have let me know something awful had happened here.

I stepped away from Chris and stood in the corner of the room, as far away from where the fight took place as I could in the cramped space. I shook out my arms and steadied my breathing. I knew what I would see when I relaxed my gaze, but that didn't make it any easier to see the pooling green goop that coated the floor. It was heaviest in the middle of the room. I closed my eyes to clear the image then turned my head to take in the rest of the room. In my dream, I couldn't look around, but I could now.

My gaze was sliding along the back wall when it stopped at Izzy standing in the center of the room mere inches from the dark stain on the floor. She flinched as I looked at her, and she wrapped her arms around her body.

"Are you—"

"Be quiet," Izzy snapped, cutting me off.

I clamped my mouth shut and turned away. As I stepped around her, I could've sworn I heard her mutter that she didn't mean me, but when I glanced back at her, she was still looking down at the ground, her body bowed inward.

I studied her out of the corner of my eye as I moved through the space. She flinched two more times while I watched her. I almost opened my mouth again, but whatever she was going through, she didn't want my input. I came to a stop in front of the only piece of artwork on the wall. It was a painting of a wolf howling at the moon. A single yellow eye stared out at the room. I breathed in slowly through my nose and out through my mouth to calm my stomach. Once I had the unease in my gut under control, I lifted my hand toward the painting and murmured the words to the spell that let me look into the past.

Izzy gasped behind me. I whipped around, and she was facing away from me, her body perfectly still. I stepped back and moved until I could see her face. She was staring wide-eyed at the corner. *What in the world...?*

"Are you okay?"

She wet her lips. "I thought I saw something move. A rat maybe?"

I peered into the darkened corner. Nothing was there. She didn't turn her gaze away from the spot as I backed away and returned to my spot next to the painting. I glanced between her and the painting. She still had her back to me. I steadied my nerves again and retried.

Witnessing the killer enter the room through the eyes of the wolf painting was unsettling. In the dream, I'd staggered and lurched about. I'd thought at the time that it had something to do with being on a boat. But the awkward steps didn't seem to be in time with the rocking of the ship. I didn't know how to describe it. He moved wrong. Some limbs bent too much, while others didn't bend enough. I tried to focus on his face. It was hard to concentrate on at first, but his face eventually came clear. I didn't recognize him. He looked so normal. His dark hair was cut short. He was tall and stocky with broad shoulders. He had a five o'clock shadow and dark circles under his dark-brown eyes. They glittered with malice as he took another staggering step forward.

Bile rose in the back of my throat, and I swallowed it. I yanked my hand away before the feeling could get any worse. I finally had a face to our killer. Now, all I needed was a name so that I could point Chris in the right direction.

I scurried off the boat. Izzy jerked as I walked past her and scampered after me. I gulped in the fresh air as I strode out onto the deck.

"Did you get what you need?" Chris asked.

I nodded. "I got a lead at the convention. I think I'm on to something."

"Text it to me as soon as you know something," Chris said.

I pulled him into a quick hug. "I promise."

I released him and followed him down the gangplank to the dock. Izzy shuffled behind me, her hands shoved into her pockets. She followed behind us back to the terminal and climbed silently into my car.

"Is she okay?" Chris asked once her door was closed.

"I don't know," I whispered. "I'll see if she's willing to open up."

"We still on for dinner tonight?" Chris asked.

"Wouldn't miss it for the world." I squeezed his hand then opened my car door and climbed inside.

Izzy and I drove in silence back to the Bizzy Bean, where I dropped her off at her vehicle. I stepped in front of her car door before she could close it. "Hey, is something wrong?"

"I… haven't been sleeping well. That's all. Insomnia is rough."

"Are you sure that's it? You really seemed freaked out back there." I put my hand on top of her door.

She smiled at me weakly. "It isn't every day I go to a crime scene."

Reading her emotions through the door was hard. All I got was the flash of anxiety she felt when she opened it. Walking around a murder scene could make anyone anxious. But I couldn't help but feel that more was going on. "Are you sure? I'm worried about you. You know you can talk to me, right? We're friends."

She peered up at me. "Are we?"

I blinked and took a step back like she had sucker punched me. My mouth hung open. *What the heck is going on?* I stared wide-eyed as she closed her door and drove away. I had assumed, after everything we'd been through together, that we were friends. *What on earth have I missed?* I replayed in my head every conversation I'd ever had with her. For a short time, I'd thought maybe she was a medium, because she was being haunted by a ghost. But she had been truthful when she said they didn't exist. Izzy didn't believe in the supernatural. If she had powers like that, she would know. We'd been friendly during all our investigations. She had crashed at my house. *Had she ever considered me a friend? Was I imagining the closeness, or has something changed?* I turned it over in my head until I was going cross-eyed standing there. The more I focused on the problem of Izzy, the more my mind wandered to other things pressing at my attention. I wouldn't be able to give her the focus she deserved until after I took something off my plate. Since I knew the face of the killer, if I got a name I could give Chris, that would be one less thing for me to worry about. I just needed to figure out which football star from the class of 2002 looked like our killer.

CHAPTER 14

The Slice of Life Diner was mostly empty when I walked through the front door, during the middle of the lull between the lunchtime rush and the dinner surge. Pop music blared over the speaker system in an attempt to muffle the sounds of construction happening next door. The diner was expanding its footprint into the vacant storefront on the other side of the wall. It was a much-needed change. Ever since Willow had joined forces with Abby from the Eats and Treats Bistro, the diner had been packed full for every meal, with a line out the door. While Abby had originally needed to borrow space out of Willow's kitchen out of necessity when she lost her bistro, I was finding it hard to imagine the space without both of them there. The decor on the walls was all Willow, and the newly installed dessert conveyor belt was all Abby. The menu had even shifted in acknowledgment of her contributions. Above the counter was one section labeled Eats, which included all the appetizers and entrées, and the other side was labeled Treats, which was the very large dessert menu, chock-full of pies, milkshakes, and other baked goods. It had become a true melding of their brilliant minds, and despite my anxious mood, I couldn't stop myself from salivating the second I walked through the door.

I marched up to the counter. Willow was at the register, with Abby somewhere in the back, singing off-key. Willow's strawberry-blond hair was in a messy braid that wound around her head like a crown. She had a flower tucked behind her ear, which jutted out at an awkward angle from her red-framed glasses. Next to it was the pencil she routinely shoved back there as well. She smiled warmly at me as I walked up.

"What will it be today?" she asked.

I quickly read through the menu. While a few classics stayed in rotation, the rest of the menu changed weekly, depending on what was in season and on the mood of the chefs. With the warmer weather, the specials had shifted to sandwiches and salads. I opted for a spicy chipotle salmon bowl with a watermelon feta salad on the side. Something about the juiciness of the watermelon combined with the tangy feta and crisp mint was oddly addictive. I was dreading the day it was going to leave the menu for the year.

"Coming right up." Willow spun and hung my order in the window.

"Do you mind if I take a look around the early-two-thousands section while I wait?"

Willow nodded. "You looking for anything in particular?"

"A football star."

She chuckled. "You are full of surprises. Let me know if you don't find it, and I can always go digging. Although, I must warn you, I have at least five boxes of photos for each of those years."

I thanked her and backed away from the table. Every quarter, she changed out the photos on the walls and embraced a new theme. The theme that quarter was Summertime Fun, separated out by decade. I located the section I was looking for and slowly shuffled down the wall as my eyes scanned the photos. It was filled with pictures of gangly teenagers at the pier, the summer carnival that used to come through, and graduation parties. I froze when my gaze landed on a photo of eight men standing in a line. They stood at attention, their arms behind their backs, their chests puffed up. Their heads were freshly shaved, but their eyes shone fiercely. On a few of their arms, I could make out a gray angel wing tattooed on their biceps. And standing in the middle of the group was a much younger version of the killer I'd seen on the boat. He had the same stocky build, but he hadn't fully come into his shoulders yet. He had a cocky grin on his face. He looked very young and normal.

"Dani? Your order's up," Willow called from the counter.

I took a step back from the wall and pointed at the picture. "Is it okay if I take it down for a second? I want to look at the back."

"Sure, let me help you with that." Willow glided out from behind the counter. Her maxi dress flowed gracefully, billowing out around her legs. She stopped in front of the picture and gingerly pulled the frame off the wall. She popped the back off and slid the photo out for me to see.

In black ink, written so neatly that it almost looked printed, was a list of names. I flipped the photo over to count the boys. He was the fourth from the right. I flipped it back. *Justin Davis.* I took a quick picture of the photo then the names on the back and handed it to Willow. "Thanks so much."

As I followed her back to the counter, I searched for his name online. Justin Davis was a common enough name, so I tried to narrow it down by adding "Point Pleasant" and "football." *What the heck?* I almost walked straight into the counter as I opened the top story. His face stared out at me. It was older, much closer to the one I saw in the memory of the wolf painting on the boat. The story was his obituary.

Justin Davis was dead, and he had been for almost three weeks.

"Is everything all right?" Willow asked.

My head jerked up. I didn't know how long I had stood there, staring slack-jawed at my phone. My prime suspect was dead. My prime suspect had been dead since before the first murder. I didn't know how to wrap my head around that. I opened the coven chat on my phone.

> **DANI:**
> Emergency coven meeting. Meet me at the Bizzy Bean in ten.

I shoved my phone into my pocket, paid, grabbed my order, and scurried outside. I strode past my car and marched down the street towards the Cafe. I ate my food as I walked. I was close enough that moving my car didn't make sense. It would have taken longer to find a new spot than to walk it. I pushed the front door open and made my way straight back to the far corner of the cat enclosure. The kittens were romping around the room. I stepped carefully over a pair tussling next to my usual table and slid into the booth. The Retirees were already there.

"That bad?" Agnes asked.

I nodded. "We should wait for the others."

A few seconds later, someone else plopped down in the booth across from me.

I glanced up and froze when my gaze met the dark-brown eyes of my daughter. "What are you doing here?"

She slid farther into the booth to make room for the others when they arrived. "I'm involved in this too. I deserve a seat at the table."

When the Retirees fidgeted beside me, I looked from Betty to Agnes to Sarah. I wasn't expecting Sarah to be the one who became flustered and looked away. "You called her?"

"Yes," Sarah muttered.

I blinked. My head was still reeling from my Justin discovery, and I felt another shifting of the ground beneath me.

Sarah grimaced. "When I drove her home from Madam Halloway's, she made me promise to keep her in the loop."

A hush fell over the room. All the patrons went still as the bell above the front door stopped ringing. Then the murmuring began.

"I can't believe she would show her face here."

"The audacity of that woman."

"Did you hear she was caught sneaking out the window of a married man's home? A few minutes earlier, the wife would have caught them in the act."

My shoulders hunched. Normally, I waited for the end of the business day to call coven meetings so that Megan didn't have to deal with the rude comments. But my bombshell couldn't wait another three hours for the postwork rush to die down, not while the victims were dropping like flies. While I knew Megan would never do those things, her curse forced people to be suspicious of her. If someone heard a story about a mystery woman sneaking out a window, it morphed into Megan Miller sneaking out the window. She'd been blamed for almost everything that had gone wrong in Point Pleasant over the years, from vandalism to petty theft to joyriding through quiet neighborhoods at two in the morning. It didn't matter that people rarely saw her off her farm. They still imagined she was somehow responsible for everything. I turned and watched her as she strode through the room, her shoulders pulled back, and her eyes firmly on our table. She didn't acknowledge any of the comments. She climbed into the booth, slid to her usual spot, and stared pointedly at anything but the other customers.

Heather scampered over after her and claimed the final seat at the booth. The fit was tighter than usual with Grace there.

Heather angled her body to keep her customers from heckling Megan at the table. "I really wish I could just dose the entire shop with the potion that lets people see you for how you really are. Remind me again why we can't do it?"

Megan sighed and slunk back, letting Heather hide her from view. "Because if they miss a dose, all the paranoia it's been holding at bay hits all at once. I don't want people showing up at my house with literal pitchforks. It's bad enough they keep painting poor Gertie." Gertie was her familiar. People were lucky she was a gentle cow because if she hadn't been, she could do some serious damage with how big she was. Familiars always tended to run larger than their nonmagical counterparts. And a larger-than-normal cow was massive.

Heather grumbled under her breath.

Megan squeezed her hand. "It's okay. I've gotten used to it." She cleared her throat and glanced over at me. "So, what's the update?"

Agnes quickly activated the appropriate spells to keep our conversation quiet. With Megan there, people would be eavesdropping. To anyone sitting nearby, our conversation shifted toward gardening.

Once I was sure it was in place, I told them, "I think I found our killer."

"That's great news," Heather said.

I shook my head. "He died three weeks ago."

Everyone at the table spoke over each other as they blurted out questions. I held up my hands and went over my day, from my exploration of the newest crime scene to my discovery at the Slice of Life Diner.

"And you're sure it's this Justin guy?" Betty asked.

"Ninety-nine point nine nine percent? Unless he has an identical brother who also got an angel tattoo, all signs point to him being my guy."

"But he's dead," Megan said.

"And Meredith was a necromancer in life." Grace shifted in her seat as all our eyes narrowed on her. "The magic was green. Her magic was the same shade. I remember that shade. If she were possessing him, it might look different. It might not sparkle because… maybe, I don't know, maybe a ghost of a necromancer shouldn't be possessing a dead body, and it's messed her up even more than she already was."

The muscles in my arms clenched. I fought to control them, but my hands moved of their own accord. I gritted my teeth as I pulled out my phone. My fingers scrolled through my contacts of their own accord until I found Warden Miranda Blackwood and dialed. Her compulsion magic wormed its way into my mouth, forcing my lips to part. It went straight to voice mail. I tried to bite back the words, but they left my mouth against my will. "I have a lead on Meredith Walker."

I sagged into the booth the second the last word left my mouth. I flung my phone down.

"Shoot." Betty hunched forward and held her head. "Did the Warden answer, or do we have any lead time?"

"I left a message," I said. "But I wouldn't count on any lead time. We have to assume they're on their way."

As much as I would have liked to believe it was a good thing that the Wardens of the West were coming, I couldn't. They might enforce the laws of the witching world, but they creeped me out. Taking them at face value was hard when they forced their will on others like that. Not all ends justified the means, especially when the means involved stripping people of their free will. I was still baffled that the only people allowed to break the three laws of magic were the ones that enforced them. They could obviously permanently alter another's mind, body, or spirit without their informed consent. And while I hadn't heard about them doing it, I wasn't entirely convinced they couldn't also violate the natural order of things or make deals with

Outsiders if they thought that would protect the witch community at large.

"Okay. So the Wardens are coming. But we still have a few murders to solve, right?" Heather asked.

I straightened in my seat. I could do nothing about them coming, but I could at least try to have answers when they arrived, so their visit would be short. "You're right."

"You know, what I've been wondering is why Vincent?" Megan leaned forward. "I mean, the medium makes sense. Any medium worth their salt would know something weird was going on in the spirit world. But why Vincent? After Meredith tried to take down Harold, I spent time tracking the family trees of the other guys he was friends with back then. None of them were named Vincent."

"Maybe he was connected to Justin instead?" Sarah turned toward me. "I vaguely recognize the name, but it's been years since I heard it. What can you tell us about him?"

I furrowed my brow. After stumbling across the obituary, I'd stopped reading. I didn't know anything about him. "Nothing."

I grabbed my phone from where I'd tossed it and began to search. The rest of the table followed suit. We called out things as we found them. It was surprisingly difficult. The obituary was short. He had died in prison. We found a brief mention of him being arrested for armed robbery, and he was survived by his sister. *How did Justin go from football star to an armed robber?* He had been in jail since 2007. The newspaper articles that covered his arrest weren't online. I exhaled and slumped into my seat as we ran out of steam.

"All right. Let's ignore for now that he's dead." I drummed my fingers against the table. "My next steps in any investigation would be to research them and interview family and friends. I doubt he had many friends around here, but I could try to find his sister. And the historical society probably has the news articles covering his arrest. I'll start there."

"And we should plan for the Wardens arriving," Sarah said.

Betty nodded. "None of us should go out without wards protecting us."

"I'll begin making tinctures that can boost those defenses some more. Just in case," Agnes added.

Megan sighed. "I'll warn Kim."

Kimberly Jones had helped us hide Grace the last time the Wardens were in town. While she might have had no interest in continuing a working relationship, she still deserved to know the Wardens were probably coming back to town.

"I'll stay out of trouble?" Grace hugged her arms to her body. Convincing the Wardens to leave her alone had been a lot of work. She was one of the few people alive who'd been possessed by a fragment of an Outsider. Their returning was even scarier for her than for the rest of us. Her freedom was always in question when they were in town.

"And I'll keep a pot of coffee on." Heather slipped out of the booth. "I should be getting back to the front. Becca's getting off soon."

We recast our protection wards and, one by one, slipped out of the booth and moved on to our assignments. I just hoped I would find something useful at the historical society. If I couldn't, I wasn't sure how to approach tracking down an undead killer, other than camping outside the homes of Meredith's potential hit list. And that list was long enough that it would be impractical. I had to find him before he struck again.

CHAPTER 15

By the time I reached the building where the Point Pleasant Historical Society was housed, I had less than an hour to find what I was looking for. I darted through the front door and marched up to the front desk.

A new girl was sitting there. Her blond hair was pulled up into a high ponytail, and her long pink acrylic nails danced across the keyboard as she typed. Her eyes flicked up at me, but her hands didn't stop moving. "Can I help you?" Her voice had a high-pitched, almost nasal quality. She could easily hit the high notes of Broadway musicals.

"Is Donna in?"

She held up a single finger and punched a button on her phone. "You have a visitor." She murmured something too softly for me to hear well then hit the same button again. "She'll be out in five."

And with that, I was dismissed. I backed away from the desk and took a seat against the far wall. The cool hiss of the air conditioning kicked on, and a blast of cool air washed over me. Goose pimples covered my arms. I stood to move a seat over and paused halfway back down as Donna strode into the room.

She was dressed much like the last time I saw her, a pale-peach blouse over black slacks. Her salt-and-pepper hair was styled into the same severe bob, a perfectly straight line from the bottom of her chin back. "Ah, Willow's friend. I take it you are researching something again. Follow me." She turned on her heel and disappeared down the hallway.

I scurried after her, fast on her heels. "I'm looking for any information the archives might have on a guy named Justin Davis. He went to Point Pleasant High. I think he graduated in 2002."

She entered her office at a brisk pace then perched on the edge of her chair as she typed a few things into her system. Her office was neat. Everything on her desk sat in precise locations, with everything perfectly lined up. She picked up a pad of sticky notes and noted down a few items before standing again and sweeping out of her office without a backward glance. I dashed after her.

Donna paused briefly outside a room and pointed at it. "Wait here." Then she was gone down another hallway.

I stepped into the room. It was a small room with a small table, two chairs, and a microfiche reader in a corner. Next to the door was a cart with a small placard above it that said Return Materials Here.

Donna didn't make me wait long. I could hear her marching from room to room down the hall, her kitten heels clicking against the hardwood floors. She marched quickly from one room to another before she whisked back in and dropped a stack of books and a few boxes on the table. She put the sticky note down beside them, perfectly square to the table's corner. "I've organized them by date. Please put everything on the cart when you're done."

"Thank you."

She nodded and stepped out into the hall. "Happy hunting. I hope you find what you're looking for."

I picked up the sticky note and quickly took stock of

what she had left me with: four high school yearbooks, four different microfiche slides, and a recent newspaper from three weeks before. Since she had organized everything by date, I started from the beginning. In high school, Justin seemed to have been a popular kid. Even during his freshman year, he'd found himself in a couple of the candid photos scattered throughout the book. I made notes of the people in the photos with him and added tally marks next to their names if they appeared together more than once. As the years went by, he appeared in more and more photos. His senior year, he'd been Prom King, was the star quarterback, was voted Most Likely to Succeed, and was in almost half the candid shots. The list of friends had ballooned, but a few appeared again and again: the seven guys from the photo I'd found at the Slice of Life Diner; his twin sister, Julie; and Vincent Callahan.

Looking through the yearbooks was strange. He was in the same class as Chris. They had played football together. Outside of the team photo, they didn't appear together again. I wasn't sure how well Chris would remember him. It made me wish I had gone to school up there instead of down in California. Because I'd only visited during the holidays or come up when my mom took off on some random adventure, most of the faces and names were only vaguely familiar. I didn't share any history with them outside of the few friends I'd met through my grandmother.

I spent too long staring at a younger Chris's face. He had his arm wrapped around his best friend at the time, Edward Lee, who was my ex-husband. *Strange, how much things change with time.* But other things had stayed the same. In the photos, Chris had a kind face, and Ed looked cocky. Those two things hadn't changed at all.

After looking through the yearbooks, I moved onto the microfiche. After high school, Justin's path was a rapid fall from grace. The first article was a puff piece about a group of friends from the local high school all enlisting in the military after 9/11. It was notable because Justin was supposedly destined for great things. But in the next article, he was barely mentioned. It was a sad story about one of the boys, August "Auggie" Johanson, dying in combat. He was nineteen. The group of friends he enlisted with was mentioned, but Justin wasn't in the group photo of the other boys weeping for the lost brother.

From there, the thread jumped a few years forward. The next article was from 2006. It was about his arrest. He was caught on his way out the door after robbing a bank at gunpoint on a weekend. The only people in the building at the time were the bank teller, Evelyn Parker, and the security guard, Jamison Brown. The photo at the top was of Justin, his hands over his head, blood splattered across his face, in front of the bank doors. A few more articles after that one discussed the robbery, the death of the security guard, and the trauma Evelyn had gone through. A photo showed her staring wide-eyed at the camera, her face poking out from under the jacket of a police officer helping her from the building. The articles mentioned that Justin had been dishonorably discharged from the Army in 2003, but no reason was stated.

The news articles picked up a year later when Justin's case finally went to court. He refused to give up the name of his accomplice, who was seen fleeing the scene before the cops could arrive. Despite Evelyn being too fragile to give testimony, the jury had more than enough evidence to convict. He was sentenced to life in prison, with a chance at parole after twenty-five years. Then nothing mentioned him again until three weeks back. He had died in prison, reportedly trying to break up a fight in the yard. He hit his head. He had apparently been a model prisoner. He was survived by his sister and had been buried at Garden Terrace Cemetery. Everything was so bizarre—high school football star to army recruit to bank robber to dead. He had crashed and burned spectacularly.

I stared at the last news article. The only mention of Vincent was the yearbooks. They had known each other. *Was he the accomplice? Is that why he was killed?* The only person who might've known the answer to that was the witness.

I pulled out my phone and did a quick search on social media for all the names on my list. His friends from high school that enlisted with him were scattered to the wind. The closest one lived in Colorado, and the farthest was still in the army. He was stationed at Camp Zama in Japan. His sister, Julie, was still local. She worked as a waitress at a diner in Oak Harbor. And Evelyn, the bank teller, had stayed in town too. She worked from home in medical coding. While I could easily bump into Julie at her work, Evelyn would be much harder. I drummed my fingers against the table, my eyes flicking up to the clock above the door. The time was almost six.

I jerked upright in my seat. *It's almost six.* I had dinner plans with Chris. I quickly piled the materials on the cart, grabbed my purse, and darted out the door. As I walked down the hall, I sent a message to Evelyn Parker through her most active social media account then jogged to my car so that I wouldn't be too late for my dinner date.

I parked in Chris's driveway with two minutes to spare. He came down the front steps of his townhome as I climbed out of my car. He had changed out of his uniform into a pair of dark-blue jeans and a black button-up shirt with the top two buttons undone, revealing glimpses of his collarbones. He smiled at me, his warm brown eyes crinkling at the corners.

"I'm sorry. I came straight from working on stuff. I haven't had a chance to change." I stared down at my jeans and a T-shirt with my company logo on the back. "I still have that red dress upstairs though."

Chris pulled me into a hug and kissed the top of my head. "Don't worry about changing. You always look beautiful to me."

I melted in his arms. "So long as I won't look too out of place at the restaurant. Where are we headed?"

"A new place I've been itching to try. It's an oyster bar in Langley. I've already requested an Uber because I plan on sharing a bottle of wine with you tonight."

"Sounds delicious."

We chatted until the car arrived. The drive to the restaurant was quick. It was an interesting-looking building, gray with a flat roof and angular features. I followed Chris to our table out on the patio, which looked out onto the water. A cool breeze swept past our table, chasing away the heat from the sun. It was perfect.

We quickly ordered food. Chris barely looked away from me as we moved through the courses, starting with oysters, then a roasted chicken leg over fried polenta, and finishing the meal off with a perfectly cooked crème brûlée. Throughout the meal, we sipped on a crisp white wine. Almost at the end of the meal, I remembered my questions about the case. My body stiffened in my seat. *Do I really want to ruin the night by asking about a dead guy?*

Chris leaned forward and held my hand. "A penny for your thoughts."

"I…"

He brushed his thumb across the top of my hand. "You look like you have something on your mind that isn't fun. Let's set a timer. We can talk about whatever's on your mind for five minutes, and then I'm going to move my chair next to you to take in the sunset. Deal?"

I flushed. "Deal."

He pulled out his phone and set it down on the table. He hit go, and a five-minute timer started.

"Do you remember Justin Davis from high school?"

He blinked. "That's not a question I was expecting."

"What were you expecting?"

He shrugged. "Something about the case."

"It is about the case."

His eyebrows rose. "Interesting. I do. We weren't close. He was a bit of a hothead. He had a lot of charisma, though, so most people were willing to overlook his more temperamental outbursts. I have to admit I was a little jealous of him getting the starting quarterback position. I tried out for it a few times but always got the backup spot instead. At the time, I was mad because I thought he had robbed me of a football scholarship."

"What do you mean by *hothead*? What did he do?"

"He was rambunctious. He had a lot of ideas and not a lot of self-control. When I heard he was joining the military, I was honestly surprised. I didn't think he would make it past boot camp." He launched into a story about a few pranks gone wrong, the most unusual of which involved a blow-up doll and a frog. "But he was just so charming he always got away with it."

"Do you remember Vincent Callahan?" I asked.

He sat back in his seat. "The guy from the boat? I… I had almost forgotten about him. He was so quiet. I think we had woodshop together."

"Were they friends?"

He scrunched up his face in concentration. "I'm not sure. Vince wasn't a social butterfly. He spent most of his time hanging out with some girl. I don't remember her name. It's been so long. None of them were in my friend group. Why do you ask?"

I glanced down at the time. We had less than a minute left. "It's complicated."

"You've got forty-five seconds."

"He died three weeks ago, and I think Meredith Walker's ghost is possessing his body to kill people."

His jaw dropped.

I sipped my wine. "Took me less than forty-five seconds."

He shook his head and collected his phone. He dragged his seat around the table and looped his arm around my shoulder. "You are always so full of surprises. I hope I get a full rundown soon."

"You will." I sank into his side, resting my head against his shoulder. I stared out at the water as the sun dipped below the horizon and the low-hanging clouds turned a warm pink, fading into a deep purple higher in the sky. "Thank you. This is wonderful. I really need it."

He rested his chin on the top of my head. "You're worth the effort. If I have my way, I'll be taking you on dates like this every month for as long as you will have me."

I smiled widely as warmth blossomed in my chest. "I love —" I floundered. The word "you" almost tumbled out of my mouth, but I caught it at the last moment. It felt right, but I didn't want to rush it. *Would it scare him off?* I didn't think so, but it was too soon. *Isn't it?* "I love how thoughtful you are."

He pulled back and touched my chin, tilting my head up. He brushed his lips against mine. "I love how dedicated you are."

It almost felt like we were saying we loved each other without the filler words between the words love and you. I returned the kiss then watched the last of the sunset. Once the air began to cool down, we stood from our spot, paid our bill, and wandered out to the street to wait for our Uber home.

CHAPTER 16

I stared up at the run-down diner from inside my car. It was even more dilapidated in person than it had looked online. The paint was peeling and sun bleached. One of the anchoring bolts had broken on the sign, and it had been reattached badly. The sign was hanging down at an angle. If not for the other cars parked outside and the busboy I could see wiping down one of the tables at the back, I would have assumed the place was closed down. It had the look of a place barely hanging on by a thread. And judging by the reviews I'd read online, I probably wasn't far off the mark. It had a solid 2.5-star rating on Google. Seeing the place, I was regretting my decision to skip lunch with Olivia. I'd left her at her office, with Charlie and her dog, Bailey, playing in the break room.

I swallowed and got out of the car. I trudged forward and pulled out my phone and held it up like I was reading a message as I peered through the windows. I saw no point in going inside if Julie wasn't working that day. And if she wasn't, I might still have time to head back and continue my morning chat with Olivia. She'd spent a good twenty minutes gushing about how happy her father—Steven Bishop, the mayor of Point Pleasant—was about the renovation of the old sheriff's station I was working on. I was acting as the liaison between the town council and the contractors to make sure the project was on time and on budget. He was planning a ribbon-cutting ceremony, and she was trying to convince me to be there for it. The idea of standing in front of a crowd that big put my teeth on edge.

Julie crossed the room to refill the coffee of an elderly gentleman sitting in the back. I sighed, pushed my phone into my pocket, and strolled inside. The hostess looked up as I entered. I couldn't tell how old she was. She had wrinkles around her eyes and mouth. Her lips were pinched into a frown, and her eyes were a dull green. Her blond hair was permed and frizzy. She had a worn look around her edges, and I couldn't tell if that made her look older than she was. Her expression shifted to a smile. It warmed up her face, making her eyes sparkle for a moment before the dullness returned.

"Table for one?" she asked.

"Yeah."

She hopped off her stool, grabbed a menu, and walked me toward the windows. Lunchtime had come, and a quarter of the tables were filled. Another woman was taking an order from a booth closer to the door. I glanced around the room. The hostess was leading me away from Julie's section.

I cleared my throat. "Excuse me. I don't mean to be a bother, but I can feel a migraine coming on. Is it okay if I sit in the back? I think it might help if I wasn't sitting directly in the sun."

The hostess veered from the booth she had been leading to me and deposited me at the table along the far wall. She dropped the menu onto the table and walked off after assuring me someone would come by in a few minutes to take my order.

I picked up the menu and immediately regretted it. A greasy film covered the plastic sleeves, and something tacky was in the bottom left-hand corner. I grimaced and read through my options. It had standard diner options: burgers, chicken strips, and a robust breakfast menu. I opted to go with something difficult to mess up—bacon, eggs, and pancakes—and put the menu down. I slid it to the corner of my table so that I wouldn't have to touch it again.

After about a minute, Julie arrived at the side of my table. She had the same dark-brown hair and eyes as her brother, Justin. But that was where the similarities ended. Where he'd been broad and stocky, she was almost fragile looking and had an almost birdlike quality to the way she moved. She smiled at me. It was a sales smile, so it didn't fully reach her eyes, but it had a disarming edge. "You ready to order, or do you need a few more minutes?" She was already reaching for the menu as she asked.

I cocked my head to the side and widened my eyes. I had been wracking my brain all morning, trying to figure out how to start the conversation, and my connection to a few of the students in her graduating class was the perfect opportunity. "Julie? Julie Davis? Is that you? Oh my gosh, it's been years. How are you?"

She blinked and leaned closer, studying my face. "I'm sorry. I'm usually better with names. What was yours again?"

"Dani," I said.

She nodded, like my name meant something. "I've been good. And you? What are you up to these days?"

I smiled. People rarely liked to admit that they didn't remember someone, which made faking a good opener for a conversation.

"Oh, you know, the usual. I moved back to Point Pleasant last year. Not much has changed around here, huh? What have you and your brother been up to? I know we sort of lost track of each other after high school."

She stiffened, and I suppressed my urge to reach out to her to comfort her. Pretending that I didn't know he'd died was hard. Bringing up a recent loss felt almost cruel, but if I acted like I knew, that might have triggered alarm bells in her head. The anniversary of his bank robbery was coming up. With his death, I could easily picture reporters coming in to ask questions if the outlet needed more puff pieces if the news week was slow.

"You knew my brother?" she asked.

"I wouldn't say we were ever close or anything. I was Ed Lee's girlfriend. They played football together. Justin was a force of nature. I swear everyone knew him. Gosh, being back in town brings back memories. I still remember sitting in those bleachers when I would come up to visit."

"Ed? Right. I remember him." She turned her face away. "Justin passed away recently."

I gasped and covered my mouth. It was easier to pretend shock when she wasn't looking right at me. I studied her as she looked away. She was half a foot back from the table. When she picked up the menu, she hadn't touched the table. I had no way to easily get a read on her emotions other than what was visible in front of me. She looked distressed.

"I'm so sorry for your loss. How are you holding up? What happened?" I sped my words up to play up the shock and curiosity.

"I'm doing okay. He had been lost to me for a long time already," she said. I opened my mouth to ask another question, but she continued talking. "You're probably going to look it up as soon as I walk away. Who wouldn't, right? Forty-year-old men don't normally just die. So here it is. He was arrested years ago. He died in prison."

"I'm so sorry." I put as much sincerity as I could into my words.

Her head jerked toward me. She shifted from annoyed to

confused. She hadn't been expecting compassion on my face. She fiddled with a charm bracelet on her wrist as she shifted her weight from foot to foot, trapped between the urges to hide and to be seen. Grief was a strange beast. Having it witnessed could either be freeing or constricting, depending on the audience. Someone who cared made it easier to bear at times. But when someone was judging the one who'd been lost, that could feel like drowning. She had expected to drown when she met my eyes, and she didn't. I understood loss.

With a shaky breath, she wiped the corner of her eye. "When I got the call, it was like he was lost to me all over again. I feel like a piece of myself is missing, and I'll never get it back."

I winced inwardly while keeping my face sympathetic. If she didn't know anything useful, then I'd come and poked at open wounds for no reason. I pushed forward with my questions, my fingers crossed under the table. "It must be so hard, losing your brother and then one of his friends so close together. That's just... awful."

Julie continued to fidget with her bracelet as she stared at me. Her mouth opened and closed, her head slowly rotating to the other side. "What friend?"

"Vince?" I held her gaze. "I remembered them being close in high school, but it's been a while. I heard on the news this morning that he was killed."

"I hadn't heard." Her eyes became cold, and she pulled out her order pad. "Are you ready to order?"

I chewed on my lip. Her grief over her brother looked real, but her expression had become guarded. Maybe she could tell me something, but pushing it might not be helpful. I weighed the options. *Perhaps a sheepish apology for prying when she returns with my food would open her back up?* I regretted putting the menu down before she got to the table.

If I still had it, I could at least get a read on her when I handed her the menu. I needed direct physical contact to pick up what she was feeling. It wasn't intense enough to permeate the air.

I gave her a sad smile and gave her my order. She jotted it down and retreated from the table. As soon as she disappeared behind the counter, I pulled out my phone and rechecked her social media profiles to try to find another entry point into our conversation. A sheepish apology was a solid Plan B, but I was hoping to find something useful. Much of her page was private, so getting a good feel for her was difficult. A few public posts were reshares of cat memes. If we were friendlier, I could show her a picture of Charlie. *Maybe the apology has to come first.*

A plate slid onto the table in front of me. I almost dropped my phone in my lap as I straightened. Standing next to my table with a plate that contained the pancakes for my order was a different waitress. I blinked at her.

"Let me know if something doesn't look right. Julie had something come up, and she had to leave. I'll be helping you from here," the new waitress said.

I glanced down at the food. While it looked greasier than I typically liked my food, it smelled good. The hash browns and bacon were perfectly crispy, and the eggs looked fluffy. "Looks good," I said.

The waitress scurried away from my table to see to her other customers. I tentatively took my first bite. While it wasn't anything to write home about, it was still good, albeit a little bland. I grabbed the salt and pepper to add a bit of flavor and dug in while I replayed the conversation I'd had with Julie. She had seemed genuinely sad about her brother. That wasn't a surprise. Twins, even fraternal ones, tended to be close. She didn't deny that Vince and Justin were close friends, but she hadn't confirmed it either. Her disappearance could have meant anything. She might not have wanted to talk about her brother to a stranger, or she could've been hiding something. I really wished I could have gotten a better read on her. While my years of being an insurance claims adjuster had sharpened my observational skills, the added insight of my divination powers really helped. There was a difference between suspecting someone was hiding something and knowing. I cursed myself again for giving up the menu too early. The stickiness of it made me want to stop touching it even though it would have been more useful to keep a hold of it for a little while longer.

If she's hiding something, what could it be? She'd seemed most hesitant to talk when I brought up Vince. If Justin and he were as close as I suspected, maybe Vince was the other bank robber—the one that fled on foot. The thought felt right in my head. My intuition often guided me to the right place, and my gut was telling me Vince was involved. *Did Justin blame Vince for something? If he did, why didn't he roll on him?* I dropped my fork onto my plate and sipped my water. *There is a connection. I know it. But what good does that do? How will this lead me to Justin?*

I mindlessly scrolled on my phone through my notes and messages. I could pull on other threads for the deaths of Delilah and Adrian, but when I tried to focus on them, my thoughts felt hollow. The pressure at the back of my head throbbed when I returned to my notes on Vince. He was my thread. He was the piece that would lead me to the answer. I knew it. But with him, far fewer threads existed. His social media was beyond sparse. His parents were dead. He didn't have any family in the area. He was a blank spot.

I paused as I read through my notes one last time. If Justin and Vince had robbed the bank together, if that was the thread, there was one more person I could talk to: the teller. I typed out another message to her, trying to entice her to meet with me. With the anniversary of the robbery coming up, maybe she would be willing to finally tell her side of the story. I hit Send then picked my fork back up to finish my food. Even with the added salt and pepper, it was a little bland. But the texture was good, and the bacon was delicious. But messing up bacon was hard.

CHAPTER 17

The night was cloudless, and the almost full moon hung bright in the sky, illuminating the backyard. I didn't recognize the small patio. It was clean, with comfortable-looking outdoor furniture gathered around a table and a grill off to the side. I strode toward the home, my gaze focused on the back door. My gait was strange. I lurched from side to side with each step. *I'm dreaming.* I stopped at the back door and peered in through the glass.

A light flickered through a doorway in the otherwise darkened home. I lifted a hand and punched out the glass. I reached through, and a jagged piece of glass cut into my arm. No blood came out as I continued to shove my hand down until I could reach the lock on the other side. I flipped it open and stepped into the house. The back door led into a small nook just off the kitchen. I strained to take in my surroundings. A bowl sat by the sink, a folded newspaper on the counter. Paper lay scattered over a small table I passed on my way into the living room. The home was warm and well lived-in.

As I stepped into the living room, the light brightened. The TV was on. A movie was playing, the volume still turned up. It wasn't one I'd seen, but the characters were in some sort of argument. I pushed out the sound of their voices and continued to focus on the details. *Where am I?* Just under the sound of the TV was another sound, someone snoring.

I walked across the room. My footsteps sounded heavy to me, but the TV was loud enough that they might not have been noticeable to someone sleeping. I stopped in front of a fireplace and reached for a glass globe sitting next to a photo. My head was turning so fast that I wasn't entirely sure if I saw the person in the picture correctly. For a second, it looked like Thomas Reynolds. I couldn't force myself to turn to look back at it. Instead, I lumbered toward the recliner in the center of the room. Kevin was slumped in it, his head lolling back and his eyes closed.

I was a few feet away when something to the right of Kevin lit up, the shrill tone of a phone blaring. My gaze traveled to the phone, and Kevin reached toward it. For a second, Unknown Number lit up the screen before he swiped his hand across it to decline the call. He sat up in his chair, wiping sleep from his eyes. For a second longer, my eyes were still on the phone when the screen shifted from the call screen to the lock screen. The time was 1:03 a.m. the next day. *No. Today. When I wake up, it's going to be too late. I have to wake up.*

Kevin's head jerked up as I took another step forward. *Wake up, Dani. Wake up.* I lifted the glass globe over my head. Kevin's eyes widened in surprise, and he threw himself backward, a scream on his lips. *I have to wake up. NOW.* My arm was swinging downward when the world shifted, and I was flinging myself upright in my own bed.

I scrambled to my knees and stared at the alarm clock on my nightstand. It read twelve thirty. I had just over thirty minutes to make a difference. I lunged for my phone and dialed Chris's number. He answered on the third ring.

"I need the address of Kevin Reynolds's home. He's going to die in half an hour if I don't stop it."

"I'll call Harrison."

I scrambled out of bed and grabbed my jeans from the hamper. I didn't have time to find anything else. "You can't send Harrison out there alone. There's magic involved."

"I know that. But he has the address." Chris's footsteps echoed to me over the phone. "I'll put him off responding as long as I can. It won't be indefinitely. But it should be long enough for us to take care of things before he arrives. I'll meet you there."

Us. I swallowed and hopped around on one foot as I got dressed. "Thank you."

I dressed faster than I ever had before. Charlie chirped at me from the foot of my bed as I passed him to grab my purse. "I'll be back soon." I patted him on his head then barreled down the stairs to my car.

As I started the engine, the text from Chris came through with the address. I pulled up my GPS and drove. It said I would arrive at 1:02 a.m. That was too close. I could be too late. I pressed down harder on the gas, speeding through the back streets of Point Pleasant. The minutes ticked off my arrival time as I took turn after turn at high speeds. I gripped my steering wheel, my knuckles white as Kevin's home came into view. I slid to a stop across the street at 12:58 a.m.

My heart was pounding as I jumped out of my car. Chris wasn't there yet. I promised him and Heather I wouldn't run into danger without backup. *I still have time. He attacks in five minutes.* I picked at my cuticles as I stared at Kevin's home. The faint light of his TV could be seen from the street. I stepped closer to the house and checked the time. Two minutes had gone by while I waited. I inched closer until I stood next to the front door, my ears straining. The characters were arguing on the TV.

Chris pulled up next to me and surged out of his car as glass broke nearby.

"It's happening." I pointed at the door.

Chris didn't miss a beat. As the phone rang inside the house, Chris kicked with all his strength. The frame cracked. On the second ring, he kicked again, and the door burst inward. He rushed forward ahead of me. "Police. Put your hands up!"

I darted into the room behind Chris and stepped around him so that I could see. My gaze flickered between Justin, standing with the glass globe raised over his head, and Kevin, sitting wide-eyed in his chair. Justin was midswing, his arm pulled all the way back. I surged forward, my hands raised, and screamed at him. Motes of light swarmed out of my mouth. Half of them sputtered and died before they could reach him as the nausea of being in his presence hit me for the first time. It was worse than the crime scenes. It was almost overwhelming how wrong he felt to be around.

Enough motes of light hit Justin that he staggered to the side. He turned his head toward me and scowled. His eyes were sunken in his skull. They weren't brown like they were in his photos. They'd changed color to the same sickly green as the magical goop he left behind. His skin was pulled tight over his features. While he'd been attractive in life, he wasn't anymore. Behind him, Kevin threw himself out of his chair over the armrest and scrambled backward on his elbows.

Justin's scowl turned into a snarl as he lurched after Kevin. I ran forward and tried to block his path, my hands raised to try another spell. The motes of light had barely left my mouth, when he pushed past me. I spun in place, my back hitting the wall.

"Stop! Or I'll shoot," Chris warned.

I could tell from the tone of his voice that Chris was saying it as a trained habit, not because he was expecting a response.

"Run!" I screamed at Kevin as I forced my will to attack Justin again. I pushed down the queasiness. My motes of light were stronger that time. More of them struck Justin.

He swayed then shoved me hard into the wall. I bounced and stumbled, landing hard on my hands and knees. He staggered forward, stepping over me, the globe clutched in his hands.

"The Reynolds line ends with you." His voice came out a wheeze. He lurched forward and grabbed Kevin by the lapel. His hand pulled back when a loud pop rang through the room. Justin staggered, releasing his grip.

Kevin sprinted out of the room. Justin growled and turned toward Chris. He lurched forward, kicking me to the side. I scrambled backward at the last second, only taking half of his strength to my ribs. Still, something cracked, and all the air left my lungs at once. I gasped as pain radiated from my side. Justin took two more steps forward, his arm rising again as he lumbered toward Chris. Before I could stand, two more loud pops filled the room. My ears rang, and I grabbed at the wall.

I couldn't hear it when the glass globe hit Chris. One second, he was standing, and the next, he was crumpled on the ground. I pushed myself up and staggered toward Justin, my hands raised to try to push him away with another spell, then the broken front door banged open, and Izzy burst into the room.

"Stop!" Blue light burst out of her, hitting the room like a wave of water. It surged over everything. "Go back to where you came from." Izzy pointed at Justin as she stepped forward. The blue lights converged on him, wrapping around his whole body.

Justin shuddered and stopped. He twitched against the light that held him.

"I said go back." Izzy glared at him, her hair wild around her face.

He twitched again as the light settled into his skin. Then he sprinted past her, out the front door.

My knees buckled, and I collapsed. I scurried to Chris and touched his head lightly. His breath was coming in and out with small pained groans. His eyes remained closed. Justin had knocked him out, but he was still alive.

"Are you happy? Kevin's safe." Izzy paced next to me. Her voice rose with each word, tinged with an edge of hysteria. "Can you leave me alone now?"

"Izzy?" I said.

She spun toward me. Her eyes widened. She grabbed at the sides of her head. "You weren't supposed to be here."

"Izzy… it's going to be okay." I gripped Chris's hand. "But we need to call an ambulance."

Her gaze slid from my face to Chris on the floor. "An ambulance? Right." She pulled out her phone. Her eyes were still wide as she stammered over the line, explaining that we needed help.

I felt for a pulse. It was strong and steady. His breathing had evened out. He was truly unconscious. *What if he doesn't wake up?* I forced myself not to think about how damaging head injuries could be and pushed myself up from the ground.

Izzy had hung up the phone and returned to muttering to someone. "I helped you. It's time for you to go, like you promised."

"Izzy?" I whispered.

She flinched and looked at me through a curtain of hair.

"Is that Adrian you're talking to?"

She shuddered and gasped as a sob wracked her body. "He won't leave me alone."

I inched toward her, my hands held out at my sides. She looked like an injured animal, her eyes wild.

I wetted my lips. "How long have you known you're a witch?"

Her brow furrowed. "What do you... Is that what the lights are?"

"So you can see my lights too?" I asked, already knowing the answer.

Her reactions to me made sense. My magic was probably the first she had ever seen.

"They're golden." She sobbed. "I'm not crazy?" Her eyes met mine. They were filled with such broken hope that my heart clenched in my chest.

When I found out I was a witch, I'd had my gran's journals to guide me. I couldn't imagine discovering it on my own. How lost she must have felt.

I pulled her into a hug.

She collapsed against me, gripping my shirt with her fingers, and she cried. "I'm not crazy. Oh God, I'm not crazy."

I held her. "No. You're not. I'm so sorry you had to be alone through this."

"I'm a witch?" she mumbled into my shoulder.

"We both have powers. It's a lot to unpack, I know. And we need to talk about this. There's so much you need to know. But I promise you, I'm not going to let you struggle with this alone."

Sirens wailed in the distance.

I pulled back and tilted her head so that she could see my eyes. "I promise you that I'll help you. But I need you to promise me that you won't run from having that conversation. It needs to happen."

Izzy wiped the tears from her eyes. "I can do that. I promise to stop running."

I hugged her again.

With my arms wrapped around her shoulders, she sagged, her head drooping. "Why am I so tired?" Her words came out slurred.

She collapsed into me, and my knees buckled under the unexpected weight. I caught her before she fell and slowly lowered her to a sitting position on the ground. I pushed her hair back from her face and studied her. Sweat had bloomed across her forehead, and her arms were shaking.

Something heavy settled into my stomach, and I swallowed past a dry mouth. *She's pushed herself too hard.* "When's the last time you ate?"

"Lunchtime, maybe? It could have been breakfast." She slid halfway down the wall, and her whole body trembled.

"I'll be right back." I surged to my feet and ran into Kevin's kitchen to rummage through the fridge and cabinets.

He must have been on some sort of keto diet, because everything was either meat, cheese, or some sort of vegetable. He had almond flour instead of wheat and a box of something labeled "fat bombs" in a cabinet. My gaze finally landed on a half-empty bag of sugar pushed back into the corner. I grabbed it and was about to dump it into a glass of cold water when I brushed past a Keurig on the counter.

Izzy was going to need someplace relaxing to recuperate. She was going to need to be around a witch who knew how to take care of someone who had used too much magic. The Retirees fit the bill for the second option, but I somehow doubted it would be a relaxing environment. Megan's place, though, fit the bill for both. But if Megan showed up to pick her up, her curse would make it so Izzy wouldn't trust her enough to get in the car—unless I had her drink the potion that let her see Megan before she got here. I shoved a pod into the Keurig machine, put the cup in its designated spot, and pressed Start.

As the machine came to life and coffee slowly filled the cup, I whispered the words to the spell that would make the clear-sighted potion. Motes of light swirled from my mouth to the cup and settled into the coffee, giving it a soft golden glow. I stirred in two heaping tablespoons of sugar and carried it out to Izzy. Her eyes were fluttering when I walked into the room.

I shoved the cup into her hands and helped her hold the cup. "I need you to drink this. It'll help you feel better."

She sipped at it and pulled a face. "No creamer."

"I know. I couldn't find any." I glanced behind me. Kevin had run out of the room, but I didn't see where he'd escaped to. As far as I knew, he was running away down the street. I turned back to Izzy and lifted the cup back to her lips. She continued to drink. Once she finished the cup, I pulled out my phone. While I stared out the window, I called Megan for help.

"What's wrong?" Megan's voice was groggy.

"I'm going to text you an address. I need you to come pick up a friend of mine and take her back to your place. She cast too much magic and doesn't know what to do." I texted her the address. "I would do it, but Chris is hurt, and I can't… I have to go with him to the hospital."

"I'll be right there." Megan hung up without any further questions. I knew she would have a million of them later, but Megan was practical to the core. She knew I couldn't answer them right then and was patient enough to wait.

I checked on Chris. His breathing hadn't changed. I sank to the floor between him and Izzy. A calm had settled over her now that she had some sugar in her system. Together, we sat and waited for the ambulance to arrive.

CHAPTER 18

I stared at my hands clasped in front of me. They shook too badly when I tried to pull them apart. The emotions were too thick in the waiting room at the ER. Too many people had sat there, scared for their loved ones or for themselves. The anxiety of it all had worked itself into every surface of the room. It lingered in the air, choking me. I forced myself to sit still and wait. If I went outside, I could miss an update from the doctors. They had taken Chris back twenty minutes ago for a CT scan. They could be back any minute, and he deserved to have me sitting there, waiting for him. He would wait for me.

I jumped as Heather slid into the seat next to me. "What are you doing here?" I asked.

"Megan called." She bumped me with her arm. "Did you really expect your coven to leave you here alone at a moment like this? That's what we are here for, right?"

I dropped my head onto her shoulder. "Thank you."

"How is he?"

"I don't know." My voice cracked as the image of him being wheeled away filled my mind.

A second before the doors closed, his eyes had fluttered open for the first time since he took the blow to the head.

Heather wrapped an arm around me. "He's going to be okay."

"When he fell down, I thought I had lost him." I sobbed. "I haven't told him that I love him yet. I can't lose him."

"First of all, he's stronger than this. Before you know it, they'll be coming out to tell you he's ready to go home." Heather squeezed me. "And secondly, I'm fairly sure he knows. He's crazy about you too."

I wiped at my eyes. "I should have told him sooner. I just didn't want to put too much pressure on whatever it is that we have by forcing the words out too soon."

"I doubt the L-word would put any more pressure on you guys than is already there. You're my best friend, but… you are a lot. In a good way. You are smart and the kindest woman I've ever known. But you're also a mom. A witch. And someone who runs toward danger instead of away from it. If he was going to freak out over a little bit of pressure, he would have by now. He's in it for the long haul." She shifted in her seat to see my face. "So, be honest with me. Be honest with yourself. What are you waiting for?"

I pulled back and hung my head in my hands. *What am I waiting for?* "The perfect moment."

Heather rubbed her hand in her circle on my back. "There are never perfect moments. There are only the right ones."

I didn't know how to respond to that. When my grandfather was on his deathbed, he told me to choose happiness. And for a while, I did. I divorced Ed. I moved to Point Pleasant. I opened my own business. I started a relationship with Chris. I told him I was a witch. But the more everything mattered to me, the more I became afraid I was going to mess something up and lose it all, and the more I started to put things on hold, waiting for things to settle down so that I could chase the perfect moment. I'd done that my whole life.

I don't want to do that anymore. I want to choose happiness. Always. "I'm going to tell him. I'm ready."

"Good." Heather continued to rub my back. "And I'll be there to make whatever fancy love-confession baked goods you need."

"Thank you." I straightened. As her hand fell to her lap, I leaned back into my seat. "Now, I could really use a distraction. What's your ideal love confession food?"

"Chocolate-covered strawberries," Heather said.

We sank into a companionable conversation, chatting about different types of food, her inspiration for the next window display at the Bizzy Bean, and the latest gossip about the boy her barista Becca had started dating. When Abby's sister started working for Heather, she had been a bit skittish after her very isolated upbringing. She had really come out of her shell over the past few months and had taken to dyeing her hair fire-engine red. Seeing someone else finding happiness after surviving a bleak situation was wonderful. After we chatted back and forth for a few hours, the doctors finally came out with an update. Chris was fine and ready to be released.

The sun was out as Heather and I guided Chris to the car. He didn't strictly need the help, but the blossoming bruise across his forehead made me a touch irrational about his ability to walk, and I had insisted on the wheelchair to the car at the very least.

"Call me if you need anything." Heather closed my door and waved as I pulled out of the parking space.

Chris sank into his seat next to me and closed his eyes. "I could sleep for a week."

I squeezed his hand. "Why don't you come stay at my place so I can take care of you?"

"Sounds like a plan." He twined his fingers through mine. "I'm sorry if I scared you."

"I'm sorry I called you into a dangerous situation."

He rested his head against the door. "Don't be. I'd do it again in a heartbeat."

We drove the rest of the way home in silence. He shuffled wordlessly into my house and up the stairs to my bedroom and collapsed face-first onto my bed. The pain meds they had him on made him slightly loopy, so I rolled him over onto his back and helped him with his shoes. I kicked my own shoes off and climbed onto the bed next to him. He turned, throwing an arm over my stomach, and fell asleep with his face pressed into my side, his feet still dangling off the bed. I brushed his hair from his forehead and ran my fingers over his temple. His skin was already darkening. I could tell it was going to be a nasty bruise. But at least he was okay. I relaxed into my bed and closed my eyes.

I jerked as my phone dinged in my pocket. Only a few minutes had passed since I got home. I groaned and went to silence it. As my fingers brushed the volume button, the pressure in my head spiked, and my eyes flew open. My divination powers liked to warn me with headaches. They usually meant something was important or something shouldn't be ignored. I grumbled under my breath as I pulled my phone out of my pocket and opened the message.

> **EVELYN:**
> I don't leave the house often, but I'm at the Slice of Life Diner right now if you wanted to ask your questions.

I sat up in bed. It was the teller from the bank, the only living witness to the robbery. If the murders were some sort of combined hit list of Meredith's and Justin's, then maybe she would know where he might strike next. I couldn't pass up the opportunity. I slid out from under Chris's arm and padded out of the room. I found Charlie in his window seat, napping. I stroked him between his ears to wake him up.

"Hey, buddy? You mind being a nurse for a little bit?"

Charlie blinked up at me and yawned. He stretched, arching his back, his fluffy white tail swishing behind him. Through the bond, he sent me a reassuring sensation as he jumped from his perch and sauntered up the stairs. He was the best familiar a witch could ask for. He sent me calming emotions, and I could sense him slinking up onto the bed to curl up next to Chris to watch over him as he slept.

With Nurse Charlie on the job, I typed out a quick response to Evelyn.

DANI:
On my way.

I splashed cold water on my face then ran my fingers through my hair to loosen any tangles that had formed during my brief nap. With the exhaustion pushed to the side, I made my way over to the diner.

Evelyn was easy to spot when I stepped inside. She was at a table in the middle of the room, a coffee untouched in front of her. She fidgeted with her napkin as her eyes darted around the room. When I claimed the seat across from her, she rose a few inches from her chair before she grimaced and sat back down. I lightly touched the edge of the table. A tingling sensation started in my extremities and moved up to my chest. My lungs burned as I struggled to breathe. I snatched my hand back before the woman's panic overwhelmed me.

"You came." She stared at me wide-eyed, her pupils dilated. She reached for her coffee and gulped it down.

I quickly murmured the words of a spell that would turn her coffee into a relaxation potion. Normally, it made people less concerned about sharing things with me, but with her, I sensed I would need it just to stop her from running out the door. I pushed my will into it, hoping it would take hold quickly. The motes of light shot across the table and settled into the cup as she continued to drink. A few seconds later, the warm glow of the spell flowed into her skin. Her shoulders dropped, and she eased the cup down.

"I'm sorry. I'm working with my therapist on my agoraphobia. It's taking a while. She thought meeting with you might help. A new person. And research projects are cool. At least I used to think they were cool. I was such a nerd." She moved her hands around as she babbled. "Although I suppose, truth be told, I am still a nerd. So is it bank robberies in particular that you're interested in, or...?"

I gave her a soft smile. I slowed my movements down. Even with the calming potion in her system, her nerves seemed fried. "I was actually looking into something else and stumbled across it. I'm a true crime junkie. A local murder piqued my interest, and I couldn't help but wonder if they were connected. The news coverage of the robbery was so inconsistent. I thought it might help clear things up if I talked to the last remaining source on the subject."

"What is it that you need?"

"Why don't you tell me your story? What happened? In your own words. And I'll ask follow-up questions if you are comfortable with that."

Evelyn nodded and shifted in her seat to a more comfortable position. She stared down at her hands, and her eyes became glassy. "My co-worker had called in sick, so I had to eat lunch at my desk. It was just me and Jamison all day. It was slow. Sundays were always slow. And it was winding down. We hadn't had a customer in a while. I was looking forward to going home in half an hour. I wasn't really paying attention when they walked in. I had snuck in a book and I was reading it, so I didn't look up until there was a gun in my face. Have you ever had a gun in your face?"

I opened my mouth to answer, but she continued like the question was entirely rhetorical.

"It's hard to describe. I've never been the bravest person in the world. All I could do was stare at it. I froze. I didn't even think to push the alarm under the counter. Instead, when he told me to start filling up a bag with money, I just did it. I was too scared to do anything else." She swallowed and lifted her empty coffee cup. She frowned at it and reached for a glass of water instead. "I filled the first bag and handed it to the other guy. He went over to the door. I tried to fill the second one, but my hands weren't working right. I started shaking, and I dropped a stack of money on the ground."

She stopped and squeezed her eyes shut. I tentatively touched the table again. Her fear was muted because of the calming magic, but underneath it was a layer of shame. She didn't like the fact that she had been so scared. But I couldn't blame her. Having a gun in your face was terrifying. I held myself still, waiting for her to continue. I sensed that she needed to get it off her chest, and if I interrupted, she might not finish.

"The guy with the gun, he… he hit me in the face with it. My nose bled everywhere. He hit me again, telling me to stop being so dramatic. Jamison started yelling at him to stop. But then there was this loud pop, and suddenly, Jamison was on the floor. I don't know where the sound came from: the guy in front of me or the guy at the door. I froze again. It was hard to make myself move when the guy with the gun told me to keep filling the bag. And then the other guy came out of the manager's office. The guy in front of me grabbed the bag, and they both ran for the door."

I blinked. *How did he get to the manager's office? Was it next to the door? If it was, why would he need to run to it?* I cleared my throat and leaned forward, trying to catch her gaze. "When did the guy by the door go into the office?"

She frowned. "I don't know. All I know is he came out of the manager's office. I didn't see him go in."

"Did he still have the bag in his hand?"

"I..." She furrowed her brow. "I don't know."

"Do you know what they looked like?"

She blanched. "I only really saw the gun. They had masks on. I wasn't really paying attention to what they looked like beyond that."

I narrowed my eyes. "Did the other one speak at all?"

She nodded. "He said, 'Grab the jewels. We gotta go.'"

"Grab the jewels? Did he take your jewelry?" The article had mentioned stolen cash. *If there was a jewel heist, wouldn't that have been mentioned too?*

She shook her head. "No."

I sat back in my chair and replayed her words in my head. If the guy at the door didn't cross to the manager's office, then there had to have been a third person. My gut was telling me Vince and Justin were the guys. *Who was the third? Grab the jewels. Jewels. Jules?* My head jerked up. "Are you sure he said, 'Grab the jewels' and not 'Grab Jules'?"

"They were moving so quickly. I thought he was rushing, and that's why he dropped the word *the*."

I inched forward in my seat. "So he said, 'Grab Jules'?"

She nodded. "Does that mean something to you?"

"Maybe." I opened social media on my phone and found Julie Davis's profile. Most of it was private, but her profile picture and the comments weren't. I opened it. She was seated, leaning forward over a table, her head resting in her hands. The silver of her charm bracelet caught the light. I flicked down to the comments until I found one that stuck out to me. *Looking good, Jules.* My breath caught in my throat. There were three bank robbers. And Julie Davis was one of them.

"What is it?" Evelyn asked.

"I just realized something." I smiled at her. "Thank you."

"You're welcome?"

"You've been more helpful than you could know. I'm so glad you came out to meet me." I poured as much sincerity into my words as I could. While I had never suffered from agoraphobia, I could understand the fear. I could feel hers in the wood of the table. Her coming out to meet me was no small thing.

Her expression shifted to a happier one. I tapped my finger on the edge of the table. She was still afraid, but blanketing it was pride. "It's been in my head for so long. It's kind of a relief to get it out."

We sat and chatted for a few more minutes over coffee. Julie Davis's involvement rattled around my head, urging me forward, but I held back for a few minutes until Evelyn's nerves began to get the better of her and she excused herself to go home.

I followed her out to the street and made my way over to my car. If Justin's kill list was the people who left him holding the bag for the robbery, then Julie might be next. Even if she was a bank robber, that didn't mean she deserved to die. I slid behind the wheel of my car and grabbed the stack of maps I kept handy in my glove compartment for tracking purposes. The profile picture was two years old, and she was still wearing the same charm bracelet she'd worn when I met her at the diner. I doubted it was something she took off. I cast the spell to find Julie Davis's bracelet. The motes of light landed on the map in a green section. I squinted down at the small text that labeled the area: Garden Terrace Cemetery.

My mouth went dry.

That was where Justin was buried.

Izzy told him to go back to where he came from. *What if he took that literally? He would be there right now.* Julie was in danger.

CHAPTER 19

I called Betty from the car. "I need the coven to meet me at Garden Terrace Cemetery."

"When?" Betty's voice echoed over the built-in speakers.

"Now." My gaze flicked between my GPS and the street. "I found the killer. It's who we thought. It's Justin Davis. I know he's dead, but it's him, and I think he's about to attack his sister. If I'm right, they robbed a bank together back in the day, and he's feeling vengeful for taking the fall."

"So it doesn't have anything to do with Meredith?" Agnes asked.

We were both on speakerphone, which explained the echo.

"I think Justin and Meredith must have made a deal or something. I don't know. But I just have this feeling like we've got to go there. Please? Meet me there?"

"I'll call Megan," Sarah said before disconnecting the line.

When I pulled up to the cemetery main gate, the early morning sun was streaming through the trees. The light danced over the leaves, bathing the area in a soft golden light. It was peaceful until I stepped out of my car, then my stomach rolled as nausea seeped into me. The wrongness that had plagued the murder scenes was thick in the air. I unfocused my eyes. Green sludge oozed out of the cemetery and was spreading out onto the street. By the silence of the block, I wasn't the only one who had noticed. I heard no birdsong or buzz of insects. Apart from the vegetation, the block was lifeless.

I steadied my breathing, carefully breathing in through my nose and out through my mouth in an effort to settle my stomach. Once I had the worst of it under control, I rummaged in my witch's kit for a bag of candied ginger I'd stashed in there earlier in case I had to inspect another tainted crime scene. As the other members of my coven arrived, I handed it out so we could all chew on a piece as we made our way into the graveyard. The last to arrive was Megan.

I handed her the last piece of ginger as she joined the group. "How's Izzy?"

"I left her with Kim." Megan popped the candy in her mouth. "I swear that woman gets grumpier by the day. I had to promise to supply all the fresh goat's cheese she might need for some dinner party she's hosting next week before she even let me through the door."

The Retirees were perfectly in sync as they turned their heads from Megan to me, their eyebrows raised in question.

"I'll tell you guys about it later," I promised. "Right now, we need to focus on what's in that cemetery. Can you feel it? That wrongness in the air?"

Betty grimaced as she rubbed her stomach. "How could we miss it?"

"I think it's being caused by Meredith." I pointed toward the gate. "And I think she's in there right now."

"Then let's go get her," Betty said.

Agnes cleared her throat. "After we cast a few protective spells."

Betty bowed her head. "Of course."

We formed a circle and joined hands. For the past six months, we'd been practicing various protection spells. While they hadn't been fully tested yet, we had gotten pretty good at layering them together. I faced Agnes across the group. She started humming, her iridescent lights filtering into the center. Once the light built up, I chanted, my motes of golden light streaking through the shimmer. The lights danced through the haze as if sewing a thread through fabric. Betty and Megan poured their power into both Agnes and me as we worked until we created a protective blanket that we placed over all of us. The lights settled into our skin, pulsed once, then dimmed as the spell took hold. With our protective wards in place, we turned and walked into the cemetery.

Our footsteps were loud on the dry grass. Twigs snapped underfoot. The sounds were almost amplified by the silence of the place. It was such a stark contrast. As we walked, I relaxed my eyes and tracked the green goop past a few rows of tombstones. It became thicker the farther in we walked, as if the trail had been walked many times before. I followed the worst of it to the heart of the graveyard, which was half hidden by a copse of trees. I slowed my pace, placing my feet carefully on the ground. My eyes flicked between the branches until my gaze landed on someone standing partway into the clearing.

Sneaking forward, I padded up to a tree and peered around it. Julie was standing with her back to me, her arms down at her sides and her head tilted up toward the sky. Sunlight streamed down onto her face, turning her dark hair to almost a honey brown. Something at her feet moved, and my gaze jerked down toward it. My breath caught in my throat as a hand thrust itself up out of the earth inches from where she stood.

"Look out!" I stumbled away from the tree.

Julie spun toward me, and I froze in place as I saw her eyes. They glowed the same green as Justin's.

Behind her, the hand was joined by an arm, followed by a head and shoulder. I stretched out blindly to the side, reaching for Betty's hand as Justin hauled himself from the dirt. Julie smirked and stepped back. She raised her hands and held them straight out in front of her. Her fingers twitched, and Justin jerked forward in time to her movements like he was a marionette.

"So thoughtful of you," Julie cooed. "All of you in one place, so I don't have to hunt you down."

Betty grabbed my hand, and Megan appeared next to me to grasp the other. We stepped forward as a unit. Out of the corner of my eye, I could make out Agnes holding onto Betty's hand and Sarah clinging to Megan's.

"Why are you doing this?" I asked.

"It told me I would get my revenge. All I had to do was help it. Why wouldn't I say yes to that?" Julie scowled. "You all mean nothing to me."

Justin lurched forward, stumbling toward us. I stared at his face. I hadn't noticed how vacant his eyes were when I confronted him at Kevin's house. But standing there, I clearly saw he was nothing more than a tool in his sister's twisted game. With a shaky breath, I began a containment spell, muttering words under my breath. Each of my coven members took up the chant next to me, our words harmonizing as we inched forward. Betty slipped her hand from mine and moved it up to my shoulder so that I could hold my palm out at our target.

Megan's red petals twirled between my motes of light, Betty's misshapen pearls, and Agnes's purple-and-teal haze. Sarah chanted the words, but the moon wasn't full, so her words fell flat. She kept it up to help us maintain the beat. I pushed the spell out toward the Davis twins. It flowed across the ground toward them. The flickering wall of light was three feet from its target when Justin barreled forward. It hadn't had a chance to solidify around him. He pushed himself through the weak edge of it and slammed into Betty, knocking her down and wrenching her hand from my shoulder. The containment spell we had worked so hard to construct vanished before it could take hold.

We scattered as Justin spun, his arms windmilling. He swung at my head. I darted back and sprinted away, dragging Megan with me. As we moved, I started up the chant again. Megan poured her power into me, and I thrust it across the clearing toward Agnes. A beam of light streamed out of my mouth and arched over Julie's head. Agnes caught it and sent it spinning back toward me with Betty's and her power mixed in.

Agnes had been skeptical about us needing to learn to cast on the run like this, but after so many close calls, I'd wanted to be ready for anything. We had practiced together as a coven to do things like that. Heather had helped us learn to cast while distracted by throwing dodge balls at us out on Megan's farm. At the time, it had seemed almost comical, but I almost wished she'd thrown those balls a little bit harder.

I took the stream of magic Agnes sent my way and directed it back toward Julie. Justin was mindless. She was the real threat. I wrapped the light around her as Justin barreled after me. I tripped on the grass and landed hard on my chest. I bit into my tongue, tasting blood. The lights flickered as I rolled onto my side to avoid his stomping foot. I gritted my teeth and willed the spell to hold as I continued to roll away. My head pounded as I split my focus between Justin and the spell. My focus wavered as his foot collided with my side. I threw control of the spell toward Megan and scrambled away from Justin, wordlessly yelling to keep Julie's focus on me.

Justin lurched after me, one hand closing around my shoulder. I gasped as his fingers dug into my skin. He pulled me backward and wrapped an arm around my throat. I continued to soundlessly mutter the words of the containment spell as he constricted my throat and forced as much of my power into Megan as I could as spots filled my vision.

Then he dropped.

I gasped and bent over. My breath came out in a wheeze as I stumbled away. Justin didn't move from where he'd crumpled to the ground. I rubbed my throat and straightened as Julie screamed incoherently from the center of the clearing. The containment spell had finally landed, and she was trapped.

On shaking legs, I rejoined my coven members. I linked hands with Megan and funneled my power into her so that she could maintain the cage that hung in the air around Julie. I swallowed and coughed to clear my throat. "Julie?"

Her head jerked toward me.

"We want to talk to the one you made the deal with." I coughed. "Let us speak to Meredith."

Her laughter put my teeth on edge. "Maybe you should try at her house."

I faltered and stared at Julie. That magic was necromancy. Meredith was a necromancer. It had to be her that had fueled all that. *Didn't it?* My mouth opened and closed as I went through everything I'd seen: green goop, green like Meredith's magic, green like Grace's when she was possessed—when she was possessed by the Outsider. Julie had said she made a deal with *it*—not *she*, with *it*. The larger of the two entities imprisoned at Meredith's home—the one that scared us whenever we poked at the bars of its cage—wasn't the Outsider, like we thought. That had been Meredith all along. I wanted to throw up. Everything was so much worse than I'd thought.

"Although, if you would still like to speak with the one this vessel made a deal with, you may." Julie bowed. "Did you want to make a deal as well?"

My mouth went dry. One of the few rules of magic was "Thou must not make a deal with an Outsider to augment your power." If the Wardens of the West knew I had even spoken to an Outsider, they might punish me as a precaution.

"No," I said.

"What's your name?" Betty asked.

I spun towards my covenmate. *Is she serious?*

Julie squatted down on the ground and tugged at a dandelion poking out of the grass. "You would not be able to pronounce it. But you may call me Demona."

"What are you doing?" I whispered.

"Maybe it knows something." Betty gave me a pointed look. "Why is it still here? What does it want?"

"To go home." Demona tossed the flower down.

"Then why don't you?" Agnes spat.

"I can't." Demona pulled up another flower. "I can't go home until I've fulfilled my promise. Or been released from it. And since there is no one of the blood who can say I'm done, the only way out for me is to finish what I started. Please let me go home. I miss it so much. Being here is torture."

"What did you promise?" I asked.

Demona stood from her crouched position. "I promised to end the lines of all those who betrayed her."

"They're innocent," I said.

"Yes." Demona stepped closer to the edge of her cage. "You are."

The light wavered as she pressed her hand into it. It pulsed as she pushed forward. The cage convulsed as she leaned into it.

I tightened my grip on Megan's hand. "We'll just have to banish you again."

Demona laughed as she inched toward us, pulling the

cage of light with her. "It won't work. I'll just come back. A promise with the Fae can never be broken."

I gritted my teeth. "We'll do it again and again until it sticks. All power is finite."

Betty came up on my other side and put a hand on my shoulder again. We'd seen Miranda cast the banishment spell only once in person. Fortunately, Harold was a narcissist, so he had more photos of himself around the room than the typical person. In the room she cast it, I had touched every object that had metaphorical ears until I memorized that spell.

The words of it came out of my mouth strongly. I raised my voice to drown out Demona as it tried to cajole me into making a deal with it instead. I moved forward until I was face to face with Julie. I shouted the last words in her face. On the final syllable, the green lights in her eyes went out. She swayed in place and passed out.

I crumpled to my knees. My stomach rumbled. The last thing I'd eaten was a bag of chips from a vending machine. That hadn't exactly fueled me for a massive magical fight. My arms trembled as I pushed myself up.

"Anyone got zip ties?" I asked.

The Retirees shuffled awkwardly next to me.

Megan grimaced. "No."

I reached into my pocket and fumbled with my keys. I held them out over my head. "I have some in my adjuster's kit. It's in the trunk."

Megan grabbed my keys and jogged away to fetch them. While Julie was down for the count now, she would be awake soon. And I didn't know how kindly she would take to us interfering with her deal. Plus, she was a bank robber. I hoped I wouldn't get into too much trouble for performing a citizen's arrest. While I waited for Megan, I called Harrison. I sat there in the grass, my head lolling back on my shoulders, until he got there.

CHAPTER 20

It was well past closing when I pulled up in front of the Bizzy Bean. Because of Peggy's insistence that Harrison do everything by the book, I'd been stuck at the sheriff's station for hours, answering questions. Peggy was still loyal to Bob and seemed to relish my discomfort. If she'd had her way, I wouldn't have gotten a lunch. Fortunately, Harrison was much nicer than that and ordered me pizza. Despite the hour, the lights were still on in the cafe. Heather was busy prepping baked goods for the next day and had asked that I stop by to give her the latest update as soon as I was out.

I paused in the doorway. The back corner was occupied by Megan and Izzy. They sat next to each other at the giant coven booth, their heads tilted toward each other as Megan spoke. Izzy stared at her with rapt attention. They both glanced over at me as I pushed the cat enclosure's door open. I slipped into the booth with them.

Izzy's face was relaxed. The dark circles that had been under her eyes for the past few days were gone. And she smiled at me.

"Is Adrian still bothering you?" I asked her.

Izzy shook her head. "He disappeared this morning."

I relaxed into my seat. "That's when we caught the bad guy. It must mean he's resting peacefully now. That's great."

Izzy shifted in her seat and looked away. "I've got a ton of questions about being a witch. Gosh, it feels weird to say that."

"Ask away," I said.

Izzy turned back toward me, and her body language shifted, reminding me of when we first met and she was interviewing people as a reporter. "Is Heather one too?"

"No." I smiled. "But she knows about us. I couldn't keep a secret like that from my best friend."

Izzy nodded. "Can all witches see ghosts?"

I shook my head. "From what I've heard, it's pretty uncommon."

"More than just uncommon. It's rare," Megan said. "You're the first one I've ever met. Although, I'm a recluse, so I guess you can take that with a grain of salt."

Izzy sighed. "I guess I'm just unlucky, then. Well, that's super annoying. I was hoping you would have a bunch of advice on how to ignore particularly pushy ones. I went to learn a few tips and tricks from Delilah. Was she legit? She told me she was going to try and help me figure it out, but… she's gone."

"She was a medium," I said.

"And that's different from a witch?" Izzy asked.

Megan nodded. "They can see and hear ghosts, but they have no magic of their own."

Izzy whistled. "And I thought my life was rough. Are there other mediums I can talk to? It's hard to sleep when ghosts keep coming to me for help. Maybe they know something? She seemed to."

"I don't know. But I can look through my warding spell book," I offered. "There might be something in there about keeping ghosts out of a space. It might help you get a good night's sleep, at the very least."

Izzy smiled wistfully. "That would be fantastic."

The bell above the door jingled as someone else came in. I glanced over as Chris pulled it closed behind him. He stared straight at me as he strode forward. His forehead was covered in a mottled purple bruise.

Megan bumped Izzy with her shoulder. "We should pick this up later when the rest of our coven is around."

"There's more of us?" Izzy gaped as she slid out of the booth.

Megan nodded and grabbed her purse. They sidestepped Chris and made their way toward the front door.

"How many?" Izzy asked.

I didn't hear Megan's response as the cat enclosure's plexiglass door closed behind her.

Chris sat down across from me. "I didn't mean to chase your friends away. But Harrison said you were headed over here after he released you, and I couldn't wait to see you."

I squeezed his hand. "Sorry I took off this morning. I got a lead in the case and had to chase it."

He smiled. "I heard. Another crime solved, thanks to you."

I was too busy staring into his eyes to notice Heather approaching until she flopped down on the bench next to me.

She dropped a plate of cookies onto the table and grabbed one to munch on. "I'm trying a new recipe. Tell me what you think while you update me on what went down. I've been dying to know what happened."

"It was intense." I rolled my shoulders. "I'm not sure where to begin, honestly. I'm pretty sure Julie and Justin robbed a bank together with Vince. Justin took the fall. I think he didn't flip on Vince because he was afraid Vince would implicate Julie, and he wanted to protect her. At least, that's my working theory. When Justin died in prison, Julie blamed Vince and made a deal with the Outsider for revenge.

In exchange, she said she would help fulfill the promise it made to Meredith."

"We're working on getting her on the bank robbery," Chris said. "Harrison's been updating me. Based on your theories, minus the bit about the Outsider, they took a closer look at Vince's properties and may have found some evidence connecting both him and Julie to the crime. And what he found at Julie's house will get her locked up for a long time. Currently, she's being held for grave robbing."

"What did he find at her place?"

"A list of names." Chris leaned forward. "Some of them had already been crossed off, but it was *long.* It started with Delilah, and then it seemed to alternate between people connected to Beau Lancaster's murder and the people responsible for putting Justin behind bars." Beau had been Meredith's boyfriend.

"Who was next?" Heather asked.

"Bob."

My jaw dropped. "Has anyone checked on him?"

"Peggy's over there right now," Chris said. "He's fine."

A buzzer went off in the kitchen. Heather slid out from her spot and darted away from the table. "Try the cookies!"

I grabbed one from the plate and nibbled at its edge. It was delicious, but my throat was still sore from my altercation with Justin. I winced as it slid down my throat.

Chris reached across the table and tilted my chin up. He hissed. "That looks like it hurts. Are you okay?"

"It's a little sore, but I'll be fine in a few days."

"While it scares me, watching you run off into danger, I love how brave you are." He put a slight emphasis on the words *love* and *you,* almost like the words between weren't there.

"I love you," I blurted.

A smile spread across his face, lighting up his eyes. "I love—"

"I'm crazy about you. You make me happier than I ever thought possible. I… I want to spend the rest of my life with you."

I didn't think it was possible, but his smile widened. He leaned forward, his thumb brushing against the back of my hand. "I love you, Dani Williams."

My heart fluttered in my chest. "I really want to spend the rest of my life with you."

"It almost sounds like you're proposing," he said.

"What if I am?" My palms began to sweat. *Oh God. This is the least romantic proposal in history. Abort. Abort.* My mouth didn't seem to want to work. I couldn't get any other words out. All I could do was stare at him.

He leaned across the table and kissed me.

"I'm sorry," I mumbled.

"What for?" he asked.

"Proposals are supposed to be romantic. And it's so soon. I just told you I loved you for the first time. What was I thinking? I'm being crazy, aren't I? I can't believe I asked."

He kissed me again. "Yes."

"Yes? Yes what?"

"I'll marry you." He held my gaze. "I love you. And I'm willing to overlook the lack of romance. For now. But I make no promises against being a groomzilla."

Happiness exploded in my chest. My face hurt, I was smiling so big. "A groomzilla?"

He nodded, a mock serious expression on his face. "While much rarer than a bridezilla, they do exist."

"Does this mean we're really doing it?"

"So long as Grace doesn't object," he said.

I surged to my feet and started toward the door. When we last talked about my relationship with Chris, Grace had said she was happy for me. I doubted the proposal would change that. "We should go home and ask her now."

Chris chuckled, grabbed a cookie, and followed me

toward the door. "Heather, we're headed home. Thanks for the cookies."

"I'll lock up after you!" Heather yelled from deeper inside the kitchen.

I walked to my car like I was on a mission. Chris jogged to his and followed me home. My heart was pounding in my chest as I pulled up outside my house. The sun was setting. The shadow of the two-story Craftsman stretched out long over the yard. Grace's car was in its usual spot, and parked next to it was a red truck that looked like Megan's. She'd probably come after leaving the Bizzy Bean. *Shoot. I should have told Heather while we were there. I was just too excited to ask Grace. I hope she isn't too mad that Megan finds out first.* I launched myself out of my car, unable to contain the giddy smile on my face. Chris came to a stop next to me, and we walked toward the house hand in hand.

A dark shape moved on the front steps. I paused. My heart leaped into my throat as panic hit me. Pressure pulsed at the back of my head. The last time Megan had sat on my front steps waiting for me, she had bad news. My mind went blank, grasping at all the possibilities. Izzy was hurt. Grace was possessed again. We failed to banish the Outsider. Meredith had escaped. The Wardens were coming. The pressure in my head spiked.

I stumbled forward, dragging Chris along with me. "What's happened?"

"I thought I would deliver the last notebook in person," the woman said.

That voice.

My whole world dropped out from under me as she stepped into the light.

"Mom?" I whispered. I hadn't seen her in almost twenty years, not since she took off in the middle of the day while I was at work, abandoning my four-week-old daughter in her crib.

"I stayed away as long as I could. I thought we would have more time." My mother held a notebook out to me. It looked exactly like the ones I'd inherited from my grandmother. "The Darkness is coming faster than I predicted. And now, we are running out of time."

"Time for what?"

"To break the curse."

Can't wait for the next book? You can get book 9, 'Charms and the Cursed Coven,' here.

In book 9, the past has come calling… and this time, it's not taking no for an answer.

After a long hunt for answers and unearthing of long-buried truths, Dani Williams faces a danger her family buried decades ago—Meredith Walker has escaped.

As the vengeful spirit wreaks havoc on Point Pleasant, Dani must uncover how Meredith broke free and find a way to put an end to the chaos she's unleashed. She must protect her town, her family, and her coven from the wrath of a woman wronged… and very much not at rest.

The only way to stop Meredith for good is to finally

break the curse. Dani must rely on her coven, her magic, and every ounce of grit she has left.

But laying Meredith to rest won't be easy, and the cost might be more than Dani's willing to pay.

A gripping paranormal cozy mystery where family secrets, found family, and hard-earned magic come together in a powerful series finale.

ALSO BY ELOISE EVERHART

A Williams Witch Mystery

Potions and the Pleasantly Poisoned

Tomes and the Tangled Trail

Divinations and the Disappearing Dead

Hexes and the Haunted House

Spells and the Suspiciously Silent

Grimoires and the Ghostly Guest

Enchantments and the Eerily Ensnared

Rituals and the Restless Remains

Charms and the Cursed Coven

A Miller's Magical Mystery

Murder Among the Hives

Murder Between the Stacks

JOIN MY NEWSLETTER

Interested in receiving bonus content like inspiration character art? If so, join our mailing list and receive access to fun things like 'Foresight and the Fateful Ferry,' and character cards. Go on an adventure with Dani and Chris as they journey into Seattle for a fun day out, and things take a dramatic turn when they stumble upon a dead body on the ferry.

ABOUT THE AUTHOR

Eloise Everhart lives in the Pacific Northwest. Her childhood was marked by voracious reading and tabletop roleplaying games, fueling her lifelong passion for storytelling.

By day, she's a dedicated insurance adjuster. It's a career that has honed her sharp eye for detail and developed her inquisitive mind—a skillset she now seamlessly integrates into her cozy mystery writing.

Beyond her storytelling ardor, Eloise is a devoted wife, sharing her home with a menagerie of rescued cats and dogs who have found their furever home in the Everhart household.

ACKNOWLEDGMENTS

I wouldn't have been able to make this book shine without the help of my editors, Rashida Breen and Kelly Reed.

Rashida, you have been with me since book 3, and I can't imagine writing this series without you asking the hard questions. With you, the mysteries always find a way to get more twisty, and the emotional moments always resonate a little bit stronger.

And Kelly, your keen eye really made the prose shine. I promise, one of these days I'll get the past perfect tense correct.

To my husband, Nate, for cooking dinners, taking care of the dogs when a writing night has gone long, and for all your words of encouragement—you made this possible. You kept me fueled both physically, and emotionally. Thank you for being my rock.

To my sister, Andrea, and my parents, I'm so lucky to have you in my corner. You have my gratitude for believing in my dream.

And to my best friend, Andrew, who is no longer with us. I will carry you with me, always. Without your bright spirit, I never would have started writing again after one to many dry papers in college. I will forever be in your debt.

"Come on a journey with me."

www.ingramcontent.com/pod-product-compliance
Lightning Source LLC
LaVergne TN
LVHW051002080826
845145LV00009B/2409

* 9 7 8 1 9 6 2 7 5 9 0 7 6 *